Twelve military heroes.
Twelve indomitable heroines.
One UNIFORMLY HOT! miniseries.

Don't miss a story in Harlequin Blaze's first
12-book continuity series, featuring irresistible
soldiers from all branches of the armed forces.

First up are those sexy men of the U.S. Army...

THE REBEL
by Rhonda Nelson
January 2011

BREAKING THE RULES
by Tawny Weber
February 2011

IN THE LINE OF FIRE
by Jennifer LaBrecque
March 2011

Uniformly Hot!
The Few. The Proud. The Sexy as Hell.

Blaze

Dear Reader,

Thank you so much for picking up *The Rebel*. This is my third book for the Uniformly Hot! series and I thoroughly enjoy writing these honorable, slightly wicked heroes. I'm a Southern girl and nothing sounds sweeter to my ears than the rough, slow drawl of a Southern gentleman. Add in a wicked sense of humor, a distinct and noble love of country, a keen wit and an unhurried smile, and they become particularly irresistible.

A ranger with HALO training, Finn O'Conner is about to make his third tour of duty into Afghanistan. Finn has never been one of those guys who struggled to find his purpose. But having recently lost both parents in a car accident, he suddenly finds himself an orphan. When the people he'd counted on the most are no longer there, Finn is at odds with the life he's chosen and overwhelmed by a sense of discontent he just can't shake. And when he runs into Sunny Ledbetter again—the one girl he'd never been able to forget—his seemingly simple life gets more complicated than ever.

Nothing brings a smile to my face faster than hearing from my readers, so be sure to check out my website at www.ReadRhondaNelson.com.

Happy reading!

Rhonda

Rhonda Nelson

THE REBEL

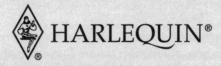

HARLEQUIN®

TORONTO • NEW YORK • LONDON
AMSTERDAM • PARIS • SYDNEY • HAMBURG
STOCKHOLM • ATHENS • TOKYO • MILAN • MADRID
PRAGUE • WARSAW • BUDAPEST • AUCKLAND

Recycling programs
for this product may
not exist in your area.

ISBN-13: 978-0-373-79590-1

THE REBEL

Copyright © 2011 by Rhonda Nelson

www.eHarlequin.com

Printed in U.S.A.

ABOUT THE AUTHOR

A Waldenbooks bestselling author, two-time RITA®
Award nominee and *RT Book Reviews* Reviewers'
Choice nominee, Rhonda Nelson writes hot romantic
comedy for the Harlequin Blaze line and other Harlequin
imprints. With more than twenty-five published books
to her credit and many more coming down the pike,
she's thrilled with her career and enjoys dreaming up
her characters and manipulating the worlds they live
in. In addition to a writing career, she has a husband,
two adorable kids, a black Lab and a beautiful Bichon
Frise. She and her family make their chaotic but happy
home in a small town in northern Alabama. She loves
to hear from her readers, so be sure and check her out
at www.ReadRhondaNelson.com.

Books by Rhonda Nelson

For my father, who was a Navy man.
Love you, Daddy.

1

MAJOR FINN O'CONNER knew his last vacation before shipping off to the Middle East again—this would mark his third damned tour—was off to a terrible start when he felt something warm and wet cascading down his bare left calf to pool in his leather sandals.

Much to his horror, it was dog urine, being delivered quite unrepentantly by a massive English Bulldog with a mouth full of crooked teeth and a black, silver-studded leather collar.

"What the fu—" he grunted, and jumped out of the way. He shook his leg, kicking off his sandal in the process, and looked around for the dog's owner. Why the hell wasn't this animal on a leash, he wondered, muttering under his breath about irresponsible pet owners. When the search proved futile, he tackled the next order of business, which was cleaning the piss off his leg.

Though he'd crawled through worse and witnessed firsthand the ravages of war, he nonetheless found this revolting. He'd gone into the service by choice. The dog, damn its admittedly beautiful hide, hadn't given him one. Still cursing under his breath, he rummaged through the back of the SUV—where he'd been in the process of unloading his suitcase when the dog had nailed him—and grabbed the first thing he could find to wash his leg off with. A shame, he thought, grimacing as he unscrewed the bottle's lid and tilted the contents onto his leg.

"Interesting," an amused feminine voice announced, startling him. "I usually sip my JD, but to each his own I guess."

Finn looked up into a pair of familiar pale-green eyes and felt a smile inexplicably slide across his lips. Unexpected delight seasoned with a startling amount of lust wound its way though him, settling warmly around his heart and loins.

The heat in his loins he was accustomed to.

The feeling in his heart, however, was another matter altogether. He hadn't had that unsettling sensation since the last time he'd looked at her.

"Sunny," he said, surprised. He'd asked her parents—the owners of the Sandpiper Inn—if she was still around when he'd booked his stay. Her father had told him that she'd moved to Savannah, some thirty minutes away. He'd been unreasonably disappointed over that news, he remembered now, and had secretly planned to see her again.

Like her parents, Sunny had been a constant at the Sandpiper here on Tybee Island, Georgia, just a short bridge and a stone's throw from Savannah. His family had started coming to the intimate motor inn when he was a toddler and they'd vacationed here for a week every summer until he'd turned eighteen. He loved the scent of the ocean, the crash of the waves, roasting hot dogs over a driftwood fire, badminton, volleyball and fishing. The whole environment here was laid-back and fun. A beachside Mayberry, complete with a no-gun sheriff (Sunny's father), Aunt Bea (her mother) and Barney Fyfe (Tug Timmons, their slightly accident-prone handyman with more enthusiasm than ability). Was Tug still around? he wondered and made a mental note to ask.

Built in the early fifties, this little motel was positioned on a prime, unspoiled stretch of beach and had stayed true to its family-friendly atmosphere. Audie and Janine Ledbetter had updated it over the years—replaced worn-out furniture and appliances— but had resisted the temptation to level the structure and replace it with a row of trendy condominiums that would have undoubtedly earned them more money.

It was a shame to think that it might happen anyway, Finn thought, soaking up the familiar atmosphere. Seagulls squawked overhead and a salty breeze slid through his hair and into his lungs. Something loosened in his chest, expanded, making him feel…lighter.

Thank God. He'd felt as though he had lead in his shoes for the past six months.

According to Audie, he and Janine were ready to get out of the hospitality business, only Sunny hadn't shown any interest in taking it on in their stead. He'd jokingly asked if Finn was interested, and though he'd initially refused, Finn had to admit that the more he'd thought about it, the less insane the idea seemed. He hadn't been able to get the possibility out of his head.

Nostalgia, he thought, batting the ridiculous notion away again. He was a soldier. He'd been through the ROTC program in college—the University of Georgia—and had logged almost eight years in service to his country.

Duty, honor and courage, those were the traits that he admired, that he could be proud of. He'd always had a keen interest in American history and particularly admired the Founding Fathers. Were they perfect? No. They were human. But their dedication to the greater good, their sheer devotion to building a better country for their children, had left an impression on him that had shaped a career. A life. He was proud of his service and, though he would admit to some strange stirrings of discontent over the past few months, he'd never once regretted the path he'd chosen.

Or he hadn't, until his parents had suddenly died in a car accident last fall.

Finn swallowed as their dear faces suddenly surfaced in his mind, his mom's kind eyes, his father's crooked grin. It was funny the things one truly missed, he thought now. He missed the smell of his mother's perfume—light and floral—and the way she used to sing tunelessly as she painted. He missed the sound of his father tinkering in the garage, the way he cocked his head when he was considering something, his laugh.

He regretted the time he'd missed with them and that regret seemed to intensify every day. The holidays and vacations he'd never managed to come home for. Their passing had put a big gaping hole in his life and had left him feeling alone and out of sorts. Uprooted. Though there were plenty of beachfront properties on Tybee Island—ones that would have been more fortuitous for a single guy with a healthy libido—Finn had purposely chosen the Sandpiper with its individual cottages and retro charm. There were good memories here, he thought, and, irrationally, he knew he'd feel closer to his parents here. It was a tribute of sorts, one that he knew they would appreciate. His gaze slid to Sunny and he took a cautious breath.

Whether she appreciated him being here remained to be seen. The last time he'd seen Sunny had been the summer before he'd left for college.

And she'd been naked.

He'd been a typical horny eighteen-year-old with a certain amount of charm, a known quantity to her because he'd been visiting every summer, and, though it had taken the better part of the week, he'd finally succeeded in charming her yellow, polka-dotted bikini bottoms off.

He remembered soft skin, moonlight and tan lines, the sound of the surf hitting the beach, making promises he'd had good intentions of keeping… and the exact moment when he'd realized he was her first. He'd felt the strangest combination of masculine victory and shame. And, though he hadn't talked to her since that night, he'd never been with a woman when he hadn't thought about her. The combination of innocence and sensuality, the sleepy reverent way she'd looked at him when she'd welcomed him into her body. The slip of her fingers along his spine. It was all indelibly imprinted in his memory.

Other lovers had come and gone—they always went, at his prompting (he wasn't called the Teflon Don Juan for nothing)—but none had ever quite touched him the way she had.

Quite honestly, she'd terrified him. He'd looked into those soft green eyes, felt his chest expand with an emotion so intense it couldn't possibly be named and, though his future had been painstakingly mapped out for years, in that moment he saw a completely different one unfurl in front of him.

One that had included her.

He'd bolted, determined to stick with his predetermined course. Though it had been extremely difficult, he'd cut off all contact, making a clean break.

Later, Finn had chalked his extraordinary feelings for her up to his idealistic teenage mentality; life then had been a lot less complicated and the world was his oyster. But looking at her now, feeling the instant stirring of desire in his loins, he wasn't quite so sure.

She was his same old Sunny—blond curls hanging to her shoulders, a golden tan, the same dimpled smile. But time had added a fullness to her figure that made her all the more attractive. She wore a lime-green T-shirt with the Sandpiper logo screen-printed over her left breast, white shorts which showcased a first-class set of legs and a pair of funky-looking flip-flops with little fuzzy balls, lots of ribbon and pink flamingoes. The shoes made him smile. Her breasts were ripe, her ass was lush and the waist between them was small enough to make her look like a pin-up girl.

The sensuality he remembered was there in spades, but the innocence was gone. *Pity, that,* he thought, and wondered how much of it he was to blame for. There was a tightness around her eyes, a harder edge to her smile. Less open and more guarded.

"I usually sip my Jack Daniel's, too," Finn finally managed to say, his lips twisted. "But I needed something to rinse the dog piss off my leg."

She snickered and mild sense of satisfaction clung briefly to her smile. Her amused gaze strayed to the animal still sitting at his feet. "You've met Atticus, have you?"

He grunted. Atticus. That's right, he remembered. She'd loved *To Kill a Mockingbird.* "In a manner of speaking. Shouldn't you tell the owner to put him on a leash?"

"You just did."

His felt his eyes widen. "He's yours?" he asked incredulously. He would have pegged her as having one of those toy breeds that could be carried in a purse or under the crook of an arm, not this monstrous muscled lump of a dog.

Sunny nodded and patted her thigh. The dog gave him one last look, as though he were contemplating peeing on his other leg, then lumbered up and waddled over to her. "He usually doesn't go off the deck," she remarked. "The sand irritates his paws. He must have been very curious about you." She said it as though it were a compliment, as though he should be honored.

As if.

Finn smiled drolly and passed a hand over his face. "I'm having a hard time feeling flattered."

Atticus suddenly emitted a loud, rumbling stream of gas that would have done an elephant proud.

Startled, Finn frowned down at the dog and a grim note entered his voice. "Er…if he's your Welcome Wagon, sunshine, then business must be pretty slow."

Sunny's lips twitched, then a soft chuckle slipped past her lips. "Come on," she said, jerking her head toward the office. "You're going to want to be upwind from that."

2

SHE COULDN'T HAVE ORCHESTRATED a better passive-aggressive payback if she'd tried, Sunny Ledbetter thought with a small, satisfied smile as she led Finn O'Conner around to the so-shabby-it-was-considered-chic office to get him checked in. She made a mental note to reward Atticus with a special treat this evening. She'd fill his Kong with peanut butter and cheese, she decided, and give him one of her old shoes to rip apart.

In her opinion, her dog using Finn's leg as a fire hydrant and the loss of a little whiskey was a small price to pay for taking her virginity and breaking her fragile sixteen-year-old heart. It was water under the bridge now—it had been twelve years ago, after all—but the first couple of years after he'd left and hadn't come back had been pretty damned hard.

Every summer she'd eagerly anticipate seeing him again—there'd been no reason to think that she wouldn't, since his family had been coming to the Sandpiper for years—only to be bitterly disappointed when his parents arrived without him.

She'd *ached*.

Sunny had read somewhere that first loves almost imprint on your heart, forging a special sort of bond to the memories. Aware that he was watching her—that his gaze lingered on her ass, specifically—she walked behind the desk and nudged the computer out of suspend mode, taking a covert peek at him in the process. Her heart, which up to this point had been racing in her chest, skipped a beat and a low hum of desire pinged her middle. *Uh-oh*. The sensation felt like a portent of doom and she determinedly shrugged it off.

Been there, done that, bought the T-shirt.

She didn't know whether the imprinting theory was correct, but Finn O'Conner had certainly had a lasting impact on her. Because she'd seen him every summer since she was a child, it hadn't taken her long to develop a crush on the bronze-haired funny boy with a penchant for pranks. But that crush had morphed into something much more powerful that last summer, and she'd loved him with all the fervor, passion and innocence her young heart could manufacture.

Though he'd never kept his promise to "keep in touch" after he went off to college, Sunny nevertheless didn't regret that he'd been her first. He was the first guy she'd ever truly loved, after all, and it only seemed fitting. The only thing that spoiled the memory of that night was the goodbye that came at the end of it. The rest—the resulting heartbreak— ultimately didn't signify.

Besides, she'd learned a valuable lesson as the result of his desertion, one that had held true with every guy she'd dated since.

Guys, on the whole, were an untrustworthy lot.

An image of her most recent ex, Heath Townsend, rose in her mind's eye, making her grimace. Because she made a habit of being the dump*er* instead of the dump*ee,* Sunny had been planning to cut Heath loose anyway. She'd known after a few dates that there was no permanent future with the real estate developer, but had avoided breaking things off with him when she should have because she tended to avoid things that were unpleasant. Heath was a salesman, and she instinctively knew that the idea of not closing the deal with her wasn't going to sit well with him.

But when she'd found out—via a message she'd heard on his answering machine—that he was more interested in the Sandpiper, or more specifically the land it stood on, instead of her, she'd coolly and succinctly ended the relationship. She should have known what he'd wanted when he'd kept wanting to spend time with her parents, even going so far as to drop in on her father. He'd been an opportunistic asshole, Sunny thought now. She heaved an inward sigh.

Unfortunately, dumping him hadn't stopped him from repeatedly calling her and dropping by her place in Savannah. The first few calls and visits had showcased a repentant, cajoling Heath who'd declared his love and intentions, but when those had been kindly rebuffed, he'd gotten increasingly more irritating.

In addition to bothering her, he'd actually had the gall to bring a couple of business "friends" by her parents' place to "show them around." He'd acted as though they were still together and the property, by association with her, would soon be his. She didn't fear him exactly, but there was something decidedly strange about his continued inability to take no for an answer.

As much as she hated to admit it, being here this week could actually be a good thing. Perhaps her absence from Savannah over the next few days would prompt an official retreat on Heath's part. One could hope, anyway.

Honestly, when her mother and father had asked her to step in for them and run the inn while they took an unexpected cruise to the Caribbean—her mother had won the trip through her local supermarket and "She'd only gone in for a Polish sausage!"—the blanket of dread that had settled over her shoulders had just about smothered her. She'd barely restrained a scream.

This place, while seemingly an ideal place to grow up, had stolen her childhood and the bulk of her teen years. It wasn't until she'd gone away to college that she'd felt truly…free. *Number Eight needs ice. Take these batteries down to Three. Six needs cleaning. Nine wants a babysitter, etc.…* It was a never-ending list of chores and, as the only child, the bulk of the gophering and menial tasks fell to Sunny.

Even now, just being here invoked the strangest feelings in her. An odd sense of peace and belonging combined with the strangest urge to flee, to escape before something happened that would change her forever, keep her here forever. People came to this place to run away from their lives—to vacate their reality—and the irony? Growing up, she'd wanted nothing more than to escape from here to have a life of her own.

And she had.

Using her business degree, she'd morphed one of

her hobbies into a very lucrative business she was proud of. She'd started Funky Feet in the spare bedroom of her apartment in Savannah—close enough to maintain a relationship with her parents but far enough away to preserve her independence—and now she had a brick-and-mortar store and contracts with many of the local upscale boutiques.

Nothing gave her more pleasure than seeing a pair of her extravagantly decorated flip-flops on a stranger's feet. Knowing that it was her creation and her expertise that had put them there gave her a sense of pride that was virtually indescribable. She'd hired two new staff members who worked to fulfill orders in the back and another full-time clerk to man the front of the store, leaving her free to design and negotiate new sale venues.

She counted herself as one of those increasingly rare individuals who genuinely loved what they did, and, though she knew it was a disappointment to her parents, she had absolutely no intention of coming back here and taking over the inn. A prick of regret surfaced with the admission—she missed living right on the beach, missed the laid-back atmosphere—but she knew it was the right course for her. Her parents could sell this place for a tidy sum and retire to their own vacation community where someone would wait on them for a change.

The fly in the ointment of that plan? Her parents weren't going to sell to anyone who wouldn't agree to keep the Sandpiper as it was. Meaning, no leveling the building and putting a more lucrative multilevel set of condominiums in its place. Furthermore, as thanks for years of service, her parents had given Tug Timmons, their longtime handyman, his own unit, so he would come with the place, as well. It was fitting, Sunny thought. Though she could easily see her parents enjoying an active retirement community, she couldn't see Tug anywhere but here. The beach had gotten into his bones, he liked to say, and he spent most of his time near the water. Rather than hire a replacement for him, her parents employed Clint Marsden, a local college kid, to cover the busier summer season. He came in a couple of days a week and the arrangement seemed to be working out nicely.

Though she knew there were probably other people out there like her parents who appreciated the old style of the Sandpiper—a single strip of small cottages with kitchenettes and individual decks, the nostalgic family feel to it—finding them was going to be difficult. It was going to take the right buyer. And waiting for him or her to come along just eked more time away from their retirement years.

Finn released a long breath and smiled at her. "Man, this place hasn't changed a bit."

For perverse reasons she didn't wish to explore, she booked him into Number One, which was the closest to the house. And to her. Clearly she was a glutton for punishment. Why should she keep him close when she fully intended to avoid him? She didn't know what sort of plans Finn had in mind, but if he had any intention of including her in them then he needed to think again. She was hardly the doe-eyed virgin of her youth and, though he still looked the part of her hero, there was a sadness around his eyes that hadn't been there the last time she'd seen him. War? she wondered. Or the death of his parents?

"Evidently, it's part of its charm," she said, handing him his key. Their fingers brushed and that briefest contact made her breath catch. *Oh, hell,* she thought, as her knees wobbled. That wasn't good. "You're in Number One," she managed to say, trying to steel herself against him.

"A real key," he said, shaking his head.

"No newfangled plastic system around here," she told him. "Words of wisdom from Audie Ledbetter— if it ain't broke, don't fix it."

Finn chuckled, the sound deep and sexy and woefully familiar. "Can't fault the logic there, can you?"

He hadn't changed much either, Sunny realized.

Certainly the boy had become a man. He was bigger, harder. The lean, rangy build of his teens she'd found so beautiful had grown into the broader, muscled body of a professional soldier. There was an inherent confidence in the way he moved; the set of his shoulders and his jaw suggested a sense of strength without trying. She smiled inwardly. He didn't have to beat his impressive chest like a gorilla to show the world he was a badass.

He simply was.

Just like grass was green and the sky was blue, Finn was lethal. Definitely somebody you'd want as an ally instead of an adversary.

Because her sense of self-preservation had obviously malfunctioned the instant she'd seen him again, she found that incredibly—stupidly—thrilling.

Laugh lines bracketed those hauntingly familiar blue eyes—a clear aqua ringed in turquoise, utterly unmatched in beauty—but a new knowledge lurked in their depths, suggesting he'd seen some of the worst the world had had to offer and wasn't all the better for it. To her regret, the evidence of war had left its mark on his face, a series of fading jagged scars across his cheek. Her heart inexplicably squeezed.

And those were just the scars she could see.

But even with as much change as he'd been through, she still recognized her Finn. The line of his jaw, the smooth slope of his brow, those wavy bronze locks and, most tellingly, his smile. Slightly crooked, unwittingly sensual, endearingly playful.

And damned dangerous, she knew from experience.

He looked up and his gaze tangled with hers, momentarily leaving her breathless. Heat sizzled through her, concentrating in her breasts. "I wasn't expecting you to be here," he said. "When I called to make my reservation your dad told me that you'd moved to Savannah."

Had he asked first? she wondered, unreasonably paranoid. Would he have chosen another place to stay if her father had told him that she was still here? Disappointment pricked her heart. "Er, yeah, I'm over in Savannah," she said. "I'm just filling in this week for Mom and Dad." And it couldn't end soon enough. She felt weird here, like an old version of herself, not the Sunny she'd become.

He arched a brow. "Nothing wrong, I hope."

She chuckled and rolled her eyes. "Only if taking a Caribbean cruise is wrong."

He laughed softly under his breath. "Definitely nothing wrong with that."

Speaking of parents…

Sunny winced. "I was sorry to hear about your mom and dad, Finn. They were good people." And they had been. Like many of the families who'd come to the Sandpiper over the years, the O'Conners had felt like family, an indulgent aunt and uncle who always had a ready smile and a kind word.

She watched the muscle play in his throat as he swallowed and a flash of anguish wrinkled his forehead. A shadow slid behind his gaze. "Thank you." He gazed out at the window toward the ocean, as if seeing something very different from her. "They certainly loved it here."

"Number Four, second week of June," she said with a sigh, looking inward. "Your mother brought me a new journal every summer. She'd said it was good therapy and I would appreciate it later." She nodded once. "She was right on both counts." She still kept a diary, usually snagging a few minutes in the early morning to jot down her thoughts. Occasionally she'd pick up one at random and thumb through it, seeing what her younger self had been doing on any given day. A window into her past, one that never failed to make her smile.

"She usually was," Finn admitted with a fond grin.

"And I could always score some Smarties from your dad. It was like Halloween every day."

Another chuckle rumbled up his throat. "I actually slipped a couple of boxes into his coat pocket before the funeral," Finn confessed, shooting her a look. "Crazy, huh?"

She swallowed the instant lump that rose in her throat. "Nope. I think *thoughtful* is a better word." She paused. "So what's going to happen to the guy that hit them?" Her father had told her the circumstances of the accident, how the driver had run a red light and broadsided them.

"Nothing," Finn said, straightening away from the counter. He exhaled a small breath. "He's just a kid and a good one at that." He tapped the key against his large palm. "He had a newly minted license and too little experience. I think living with what he's done is going to be punishment enough. I damned sure don't envy him that."

Mercy was an underappreciated virtue, Sunny thought, her throat suddenly tight. She hoped that boy recognized it enough to be able to pay it forward one day. He was probably too young to fully appreciate the gift that Finn had given him, but with maturity would come wisdom and possibly gratitude.

She merely nodded, not sure what to say. Thankfully, they both heard Atticus break the increasing silence in his usual way—by breaking wind—and they chuckled.

Finn's eyes widened and his face crumpled in disgust as the scent rose. "Geez, dog. Is this a chronic problem?"

She shushed him with a feigned frown and, out of habit, squirted some lemon-scented freshener into the air. "He can't help it."

Finn aimed a skeptical look at Atticus. "Does he try?"

"Probably not," she admitted with a smile. "But he's mine and I love him."

His gaze bumped into hers and the atmosphere instantly changed between them. Became charged, almost static. The air in her lungs thinned and a snake of heat wound through her limbs. "Lucky dog," he murmured, his eyes dropping to her lips, making them tingle.

Sunny inhaled a shaky breath. And on that note, it was time for her to go. She needed to clean the pool or check the ice machine or something. The last damned thing she needed to do was get involved on any level with Finn O'Conner. He was a walking expiration date, as fleeting as smoke. A hit-and-run-romance waiting to happen.

A more progressive-thinking woman might simply take advantage of that, adopt the enjoy-it-while-it-lasts mentality. And if it were any other guy but Finn, who was to say she wouldn't? It wasn't like she'd never had the occasional one-night stand. But it *was*

Finn and Sunny didn't trust herself enough to not let her heart get involved. This guy, for whatever reason, was her Achilles' heel. Her gaze moved over him once again, taking in the unequalled magnificence of the man he'd grown into and she felt a bolt of sheer lust land in her belly and drift south, warming parts of her that were better left alone. Just looking at his mouth made a vision of those talented lips slipping down her throat suddenly surface in her mind's eye, causing her heart to skip a beat in her chest.

She grimly suspected she was going to have to trade in her feisty flip-flops for a pair of combat boots.

An irrational surge of terror speared through her, jolting her into action. Honestly, between being here at the inn and seeing Finn again, she was feeling increasingly out of sorts.

"So you're here until Friday?" she asked, coming around the desk. She inwardly winced at the sound of her voice. It was too high, too happy. Shrill even.

Something shifted behind those too-perceptive eyes. "I am."

"Well, we're pleased you chose the Sandpiper for your vacation stay," she said briskly, the official spiel they routinely gave the newcomers. Not that they had many. Once people stayed here, they typically came back, just like Finn and his family and the various other tenants here at the moment. She felt an especially bright smile stretch across her face, but couldn't seem to stop it. "If you need anything, just let me know."

Recognizing the dismissal for what it was, Finn stilled and gave her a curious look—one that was eerily discerning. He'd always been able to do that, damn him. Peer right into her brain and pluck out her thoughts. When they were younger, she'd thought it romantic. She'd fancied that he was the only guy who could open a window to her soul.

Time to close the shutters.

Sunny turned and stepped to the door. She was almost through it when Finn said, "It's really good to see you again, Sunny. Can we catch up later?" She could hear the grin she loved in his voice—the slow, sexy, playful one. The one that made her want to kiss the corner of his mouth. "I'll share what's left of my Jack."

Swearing emphatically under her breath, she squeezed her eyes shut, pasted a smile back on her face and reluctantly turned around. If she said no it would look bad. Like she was still angry at him for what had happened, which would make her look pathetic for holding on to a grudge for a dozen years.

But if she said yes, he might perceive it as the green light for another vacation tryst. She wasn't blind. She'd seen the interest flare in those mesmerizing eyes and, while it was more gratifying than she could have ever imagined, she'd be a fool to respond to it.

Finn O'Conner was a slippery slope. And, while the idea of slipping and sliding all over him might hold vast physical appeal—she inwardly shivered at the thought—it was a very bad idea.

An idea of *epically* bad proportions.

She hesitated, torn.

"Come on, Sunny," he cajoled, adding an additional dose of charm to his smile. As if it wasn't lethal enough already. "It'll be good to catch up."

"Sure," she finally agreed, not seeing a way out of it. But beyond tonight he was on his own. She couldn't afford to get tangled up with Finn O'Conner again. He was every bit as temporary now as he'd been at eighteen. And she grimly suspected her heart wouldn't fare any better than it had the last time.

What was that old saying? Fool me once, shame on you. Fool me twice, shame on me.

She'd already been his fool once. She hadn't regretted it then, but something told her it would be a different story this time around.

"Morning, Martha Ann," Tug Timmons said with a deferential nod. "How are you on this glorious summer day?"

Martha Ann Bradford looked up from the romance novel she was reading and, silently cursing the rush of pleasure merely hearing his voice brought, sent him a look and smiled sweetly. "I'd be a lot better, Tug, if you weren't standing on my foot."

He blinked, then leaped back. A red flush crept beneath his tanned skin and those bright-blue eyes— the exact shade of the sky this morning, she noted— darkened with chagrin. "Sorry," he murmured. "Are you okay?"

She'd be a helluva lot better if he'd quit being so nice. How the heck was she supposed to fall gracefully into her dotage and enjoy her retirement if he was making her feel like a schoolgirl again, complete with her first crush. She'd spent entirely too much time in front of the mirror this morning and had been pretty heavy-handed with the anti-wrinkle cream. Such foolishness at her age.

Martha Ann didn't want to like Tug. In the first place, she'd only been widowed a year and in the second place, she was certain her kids wouldn't approve. They wanted her to plant flowers and make sugar cookies and dust the picture of their father on the mantel. She was sixty-eight—a youthful sixty-eight, she would admit—but the time for romance had past.

Unfortunately, her libido didn't agree.

In fact, she'd suspected her libido had died long before her husband and it was quite disconcerting to discover otherwise.

"I'm grilling steaks this evening," he told her, his voice low and smooth. "I thought you might like to come down for dinner."

Martha Ann smiled, unable to help herself. "Don't you grill steaks every evening, Tug?" she asked. He'd proffered the same question every morning since she'd arrived two weeks ago. She and her late husband, Sheldon, had been coming to the Sandpiper every summer for the past ten years. She'd noticed Tug, of course. He was fit from working at the inn, he had a smile that was warm and genuine and he never failed to make some positive comment about her hair, her outfit, her pedicure, whatever.

After years of being practically invisible and listening to constant criticism from her husband, she'd be lying if she said she hadn't preened a little when he paid her a compliment. But she'd been safely married then and hadn't allowed herself any unseemly thoughts.

But she wasn't married anymore. And the unseemly thoughts were beginning to get the better of her. She heaved a mental sigh.

It would be so much easier if he'd stop being nice to her.

Tug chuckled, the sound welcome and curiously intimate against her ears. "Not every night, no," he said. "Just the nights I invite you to dinner. What do you say, Martha Ann?" He frowned as a thought struck. "You're not a vegetarian, are you?"

She felt her lips twitch. "No."

"Are you off red meat?"

"No."

"Then come to dinner," he said. "I'll take care of everything."

She suspected he would. And she would like it. Too much. Martha Ann sighed again. "I'd better not," she told him. "I'm working on something." A puzzle. How exciting. Maybe after she'd completed it, she'd do something really thrilling like a crossword or a paint-by-number kit.

Though she knew he was disappointed, he was too much of a gentleman to let it show. He merely nodded and smiled at her, almost knowingly, as though he knew what she was afraid of. "Maybe another time, then," he said.

And with that parting comment, he moved on, ambling along the beach, his bare feet in the surf.

Martha Ann ignored the regret that weighted her middle and determinedly settled in with her book once more. She was widowed, she was retired and, like it or not, this was what was expected of her.

Pity that she hated it.

3

IT WAS A RELUCTANT YES, but a yes all the same, Finn thought as he watched Sunny disappear around the side of the building, Atticus a big wad of furry muscle on her heels. He shook his head, the sight of them together making him smile. Though it was difficult, he resisted the irrational urge to follow her, to go ahead and tender the apology he owed her now rather than waiting until later.

Though he had a reputation for being a little reckless—he had a hair-trigger temper and an affinity for doing things his own way, conventional or not—Finn didn't function without an agenda. He always had a purpose and, though one would think that he'd go into a vacation without one, one would think *wrong*. While the locale of his retreat had been decided when he'd been flipping through old family photographs after his parents' death, it was the only impromptu decision he'd made, one that had immediately felt right.

Finn had good instincts—it was no small part of what had made him a good soldier—and he'd learned to listen to his gut. Some of the happiest memories of his childhood had been spent here with his family—fishing with his dad, picking up shells with his mother, hanging out with Sunny. He'd ripped and romped from one end of this beach to the other and had enjoyed every single minute of it.

Furthermore, though it might sound a bit bizarre, Finn had always had a thing for water. He loved the crash of the surf, the smell of the ocean, the sound of it hitting the beach. It soothed him in a way that was hard to describe, to put into mere words. When he was a kid he used to stand in the surf and draw a direct imaginary line from where he was to beyond the horizon, then would run and look at the globe to see what body of land that line would encounter next and marvel at the expanse. He chuckled, remembering.

Coming here had been a no-brainer.

But coming here didn't change what he was supposed to do. He'd soon be starting his third tour of duty in five years—this time to Afghanistan—and getting his head ready for war was his first priority.

An Army Ranger did *not* go into enemy territory

without preparation, particularly not one like himself who often found himself on covert ops.

With that in mind, his second order of business was to try and figure out what had brought on this burgeoning sense of discontent. It would be easy to see his parents' death as the reason behind this pressing urge to reevaluate his life, to step back and reassess, to see if his priorities needed to shift, but ultimately, he knew that wasn't true. He'd felt this coming on now for some time. Seeing fellow soldiers moon over a picture of their wife and kids had never bothered him before, but now he found himself turning away, unable to look at their happiness without a strange pang echoing in the empty pit of his stomach.

Overhearing the occasional intimate conversation—the I love yous and I miss yous, a father reading a story over the phone to his kid five thousand miles away, the soft intimate chuckle of a guy talking to the woman he loved... None of that had ever mattered to him. It was part of the scenery and par for the course. Honestly, he'd always been above it, for a lack of better description, operating on a less complicated playing field than the rest of them. In some sense, he'd even pitied them. He'd been solely focused on the job, utterly intent on being a soldier, doing his absolute best.

And those things were still important—Finn O'Conner didn't do anything half-assed and never would. It was all or nothing.

But he had to admit that there was an ever-expanding hole in his gut that was making him feel emptier by the minute. Whether he was experiencing a really early midlife crisis that would pass or a genuine sense of discontent that wouldn't be remedied without action remained to be seen. Whether the idea of owning the Sandpiper and carving out a new life—one that would better accommodate a family, if that ended up being what he wanted—was simply a product of essentially being orphaned or of a sense of nostalgia, he wasn't sure.

But, one way or another, he would know by the end of the week.

In all honesty, other than that one night all those years ago on the beach with Sunny, Finn had never imagined that he'd ever tick anything but "single" on his tax return. He'd wanted to be a soldier since he was old enough to play with the little plastic kind, and that desire had only grown as he'd gotten older. By the time he'd been ready to start college, it had hit fever pitch. He'd determinedly resisted the urge to contact Sunny after he'd left and had quickly leaped into the dating scene at the U of G. It was there that he'd earned the "Teflon Don Jaun" moniker and the nickname had been with him since.

Nothing ever stuck to him, most certainly not a woman.

Going the whole family route had never held any appeal for him. And, while he wasn't certain it was more palatable now, he also couldn't deny that the idea had been slowly circling in the back of his brain. As his father had always been quick to point out, he was the last of their O'Conner line. There was something unaccountably sad about that, Finn thought, and if he had children now, they'd never know their grandparents. The thought made his throat constrict, forcing him to swallow. That the O'Conners had lasted for centuries—through famine and disease, in wealth and in hardship—and would ultimately end with him.

By choice?

Furthermore, when he'd decided to come back to the Sandpiper, he'd also put another thing on his to-do list. He'd resolved to man-up and apologize to Sunny. It was a long time coming, he knew, but better late than never, he'd hoped. When he'd found out that she wouldn't be here, Finn had realized just how important righting that old wrong had become to him. So much so that he'd planned on getting her address from her parents and making the short drive over to Savannah.

How fortuitous that she was here.

His blood quickened and the telltale burn of desire seared through his veins, but Finn determinedly beat it back, grimly noting that it was more difficult to do that than usual. He had plenty to occupy his mind this week—readying for war and evaluating potentially life-changing decisions.

Seducing Sunny Ledbetter was nowhere on the list.

He'd do well to remember that.

Resolved to that course, he made quick work of unloading his gear and moved everything into his room. This one had a double bed, covered with a pale blue spread. A love seat with two shell-shaped pillows sat in front of an entertainment center and various watercolor beach scenes decorated the walls. He was particularly drawn to one. It depicted a young boy and a girl—the boy bronze-haired, the girl blond— holding hands on the beach, their backs to the artist, feet in the surf. They looked strangely familiar. Upon closer inspection, he realized why and the knowledge made another knot form in his throat.

The artist was his mother and the subjects? Him and Sunny. He couldn't have been more than ten, probably younger, he thought, leaning forward to get a better look. Had Sunny put him in here on purpose? Finn wondered. So he would see the painting? If so, he appreciated it. It was nice to know that a part of his parents remained here, in a place they'd cared so much about. He could remember them dancing on the deck, his dad giving his mom a slow twirl. His mother's smile when she wound up back in his father's arms. He remembered his mother cooking breakfast at the stove, his dad kissing her cheek. They'd always been an affectionate couple, never afraid to demonstrate their feelings.

It was only as an adult that he could appreciate just how rare that was, how happy they'd truly been.

Finn passed a hand over his face and looked around, noting some of the other changes. The old Formica countertops in the kitchen had been re-placed with a modern shiny black laminate and the appliances were relatively new. The familiar scents of lemon cleaner and salty air triggered a sense of homecoming he hadn't expected, making a smile crawl across his lips.

Strangely energized, he made quick work of set-tling in. Within minutes his clothes were on hangers, his shoes in the closet and everything else was packed away in the drawers. He'd stopped on the way in at a little grocery store, stocking up on drinks, snacks and different things to grill. Finn was of the opinion that any meat was better when it was cooked over an open flame. He'd bought a new beach chair and a cooler and soon had both on the sand, his feet in the surf. Armed with a packet of peanuts and a cold beer, Finn sighed and rested more firmly into his seat.

Now *this* was what he called a vacation.

He watched a sailboat bob around in the distance, a boy paddle out on a surfboard. Down the beach, a couple of kids were building a sand castle, being overseen by what he imagined were their grandparents. He drummed his fingers on the chair and looked in the other direction.

More of the same.

He sighed and took a mouthful of beer. Popped a few peanuts into his mouth. Watched the water shift the little bits of shell around his feet, the rhythmic move of the ocean as it returned over and over, eroding the sand beneath his heels. He looked over his shoulder, hoping to catch a glimpse of Sunny, or even her horrid farting dog.

He saw neither.

Yes, he was officially on vacation, Finn thought. And with a dawning sense of dread, he realized… he was bored to death.

Shit.

THOUGH SHE WAS TRYING not to be too aware of him—quite futilely, of course—Sunny found herself looking out the window at Finn for the rest of the afternoon. She'd seen him take his chair and cooler down to the beach and had expected him to sit in the sun for several hours until it was time for them to "catch up" as he'd put it.

Interestingly, he hadn't.

He'd gone for a walk, stopped and talked to fellow vacationers, taken surfing lessons from Jamie, a kid from South Carolina whose family was staying in Number Nine and, most recently, she'd watched him help the Morrison twins—more guests of the inn—build a moat around their sand castle.

He had no idea how to be still, Sunny realized and wondered exactly when he'd forgotten how. In summers past, he would have spent hours with his toes in the water, simply…being.

Clearly, she wasn't the only one who'd changed.

But the inn certainly hadn't, she thought, watching the activity on the decks in front of the cottages, the families playing on the sand and in the ocean. Teenagers played volleyball and tossed Frisbees, children toted buckets of water to their sand castles and played in the surf. Laughter and music floated to her on the salty breeze, inexplicably pushing a smile over her lips.

A man suddenly poked his head into the office. "Mrs. Ledbetter?"

She wasn't expecting anyone else and, as usual, they were fully booked. "I'm Ms. actually. The Mrs. is on a cruise. Can I help you?"

"Ah, it's nice to finally meet you. I'm Victor Henniger," he said, as if she should know the name. He smiled a bit bashfully. "I hope that I'm not being too presumptuous, but was hoping I could take a look around."

For whatever reason, an alarm bell sounded in the back of Sunny's mind. She winced regretfully. "I'm afraid that we're full," she said. "But I'd be happy to take your number in the event of a cancellation."

His own smile turned uncertain. "Oh, I don't need a room. I just wanted to check out the property out before the surveyors arrived."

"Surveyors?" she said. "Who did you say you were again?" Her parents hadn't mentioned scheduling a survey. Furthermore, a survey for what?

"I'm Victor Henniger," he told her again. "Your fiancé is coordinating the sale of the property between myself and your parents."

Her fiancé? She blinked and gave her head a shake. "Er, I'm not engaged and my parents aren't selling the Sandpiper."

He frowned and raised a brow. "You're not en-gaged to Heath Townsend?"

Sunny felt her expression blacken. "No, I'm not, Mr. Henniger. And I don't know exactly what he's told you about the inn, but it's not for sale. Even if it were, he certainly wouldn't be brokering a deal on behalf of my parents."

Honestly, the nerve of the man! She'd like to lit-erally squeeze his head right off his shoulders. He'd ordered a survey? Had he lost his mind? She knew he'd been behaving bizarrely, but this… This took the cake.

Mr. Henniger grew thoughtful for a moment, seemingly as perplexed as she'd been a moment ago and he smiled an apology, then gave a helpless shrug. "I'm very sorry for bothering you. Clearly, I've been misinformed."

That was a nice way of saying he'd been lied to, Sunny thought as she watched the man leave. Damned Heath. Did the truth even know how to come out of his mouth?

Satisfied that all her arrivals were in for the day, Sunny closed up the office and hurried over to the house to freshen up a bit before she met Finn. Though she hadn't lived here in years, the house still smelled familiar, like cinnamon buns and furniture polish. The tongue-and-groove ceilings had a new coat of white paint and the gleaming hardwood floors were covered in various rugs. Her mother had been collecting sea glass for years—bits that had washed ashore—and she'd displayed them in clear jars on the windowsill in the kitchen. Her father had the same affinity for old globes, which lined the bookcases on either side of the fireplace in the living room.

Everywhere she looked she saw her parents, bits of their personalities, a lifetime of living, loving and laughing in this old house. She breathed in the familiar sounds and smells and felt a little bit of her soul sigh. She'd moved away ten years ago and was utterly content with her apartment in Savannah, the life she'd carved out for herself. But she had to admit it was nice to come home. Nice that she could think of it that way now.

Because this place, no matter where she lived, was always going to be home.

That probably wasn't a good thing, since she had no intention of ever moving back. She'd made her life and she was happy. She loved her business, loved having her independence. *You could have that here, too,* a little voice whispered in the back of her brain. *You'd be happy.* Determinedly ignoring the wayward thoughts, she sighed and hurried upstairs to her old room.

Though she didn't want to encourage Finn in any

way, Sunny was just vain enough to want to look good. She resisted the urge to change into something more flattering—too obvious—but tidied her hair and makeup and spritzed on a bit of cologne. Atticus promptly sneezed, sending peanut-butter-scented slobber all over her leg.

Oh, goody.

Used to his excessive spit and to having it routinely wiped and spewed upon her, Sunny merely heaved a beleaguered sigh and washed it off. She clipped the leash onto the dog collar, grabbed his water bowl and a flip-flop for him to chew on, then made her way back over to the inn.

The sun was sinking low on the horizon, casting orange sparkles over the waves. Tug was playing Otis again—"(Sittin' On) The Dock of the Bay"—and was sitting outside on his deck tying fishing lures. She waved at him, but he didn't see her. The beach was alive with guests going about their evening activities. The sizzle of meat hitting a hot grill, the smell of shrimp boiling in spicy water, children flying kites and laughing, the occasional admonition from a parent. Though she wouldn't have believed it even a day ago, Sunny had to admit that she'd missed this. The beach, the way of life, was in her blood. Though she liked to be busy, she appreciated the pace of life around here and had carried it with her to Savannah.

Finn was waiting for her on the deck, a smile on his sinfully sculpted lips. That little smile sent a dart of heat straight to her womb. He wasn't sitting, of course—he seemed incapable of that now—but rather leaning against the railing. Good Lord, he looked good. Not just good, but absolutely freaking fantastic. A coil of heat tightened in her middle and she had the inexplicable urge to walk up to him and kiss the living hell out of him, to taste him and breathe him in. He'd already gotten a bit of sun and it gleamed on his nose and cheeks.

Despite the military cut, his hair still had a bit of wave to it and she loved the way it curled at the nape of his neck and around his ears. He wore a pair of khaki shorts that clung dangerously low on his lean hips and a navy blue T-shirt. His feet were bare, which she found ridiculously sexy. He'd showered before she'd come over and the scent of some musky fragrance rose off his skin. It was intoxicating and made her want to lick him all over. While he was naked.

It was criminally unfair.

He glanced at Atticus and raised a brow. "You're not expecting me to fill that bowl with Jack, are you?

Given his digestion problems, I can tell you that I wouldn't recommend it."

"He prefers champagne," Sunny quipped, mounting the steps. She let go a shaky breath and fastened the leash to the deck, then tossed the dog the shoe. Atticus immediately snatched the hot-pink flip-flop up and began tearing it into bits. She rolled her eyes, a wave of affection running through her. "It's for his water," she said. "He's always thirsty."

He shot her animal a skeptical glance. "He sure looks like a high-maintenance dog."

Determinedly ignoring the sizzle of awareness that tingled along her nerve endings, she slipped inside and quickly filled the bowl, then rejoined him on the deck. He had a tumbler waiting on her when she returned, and his fingers brushed hers when he handed it to her. Deliberately, she thought.

Eek. This was going to be harder than she thought.

"He *is* a high-maintenance dog," she said. Did that strangled voice belong to her? Sheesh. "His previous owners couldn't handle the stress."

He settled into one of the Adirondack chairs and kicked his feet out. His legs were longer than she remembered. Had more muscle definition. Her mouth suddenly went dry. "You haven't had him since he was a puppy?"

Sunny struggled to focus, tried to forget the bed mere feet away. "He was still a puppy when I got him, a very gassy one," she said, laughing.

"So you found him at a shelter?"

"I did," she confirmed with a nod. "I'd actually picked out a little poodle mix—chocolate with sweet brown eyes—from the website. A good dog for apartment living. Small, relatively inexpensive to feed. I'd considered all the options, determined to make the right choice." She took a sip of her drink, appreciating the burn. "I walked in to get a little dog and came out with Atticus. He's a purebred, you know," she added. "But he gnaws on everything, slobbers even worse and could win an international farting contest hands down."

Finn chuckled, the sound smooth and sexy. Intimate. *Damn.* Want, need and pure sexual desire swirled through her, settling hotly in her sex. "In other words, no one was lining up to take him home."

She swallowed. "He was a misfit and he was lonely. I couldn't leave him there."

"And the poodle mix?"

"Was adopted before I finished the paperwork for Atticus," she told him. She took another sip, savoring the flavor. "The cute dogs never lack for homes. It's the ugly ones that get passed over."

Finn reached down and slid a large hand over Atticus's wrinkled head. She found herself unreasonably jealous of her dog and imagined that big hand skimming down her back. "He's got some personality issues, but he's sure as hell not ugly."

Pleased, she smiled. Heath had hated her dog to the point that he couldn't appreciate anything about him. Atticus hadn't cared for him either, which should have been a clue to his true character.

He leaned back and released a big breath. "So your mom and dad are cruising the Caribbean and you're here?"

"That about sums it up, yes."

"So what do you do when you're not here?"

She shrugged. "Hook mostly. I've been working a corner downtown for years."

Finn choked on his drink and a wheezing laugh rattled up his throat. She'd missed that sound, Sunny realized, chuckling, too.

"That was evil," he told her, seemingly impressed, his eyes watering.

"Sorry." She shrugged. "Couldn't resist."

She loved the way his eyes crinkled around the corners when he smiled. "So when you're not hooking, what do you do?"

She held her feet up and wiggled them significantly. "I design flip-flops."

He stared at her, his expression blank. "You're yanking my chain again."

"I'm not," she insisted, laughing. "I started playing around with them when I was still in high school, actually sold them from the front office here in the beginning. More and more people started calling me, asking for designs to go with specific outfits—the bridal ones were particularly good sellers—and the rest is history." She pushed her hair away from her face. "I got my business degree, started a web business first, then went brick and mortar. I've got a store in Savannah." And if she sounded proud of herself, it was because she was. She loved her business and knew she was good at it.

"That's incredible, Sunny," he said with a wondering shake of his head. A slow grin slid across his lips. "And sort of ironic coming from a girl who never wore shoes."

Too true, she knew. "Ah, but if you remember, when I did wear shoes, I wore flip-flops. They were always my first choice."

He laughed. "Only because you could get in and out of them so quickly."

"And the sand didn't collect in them the way they did sneakers."

"I'm happy for you," he said, sincerity ringing in

his voice. "That's awesome. No wonder you don't want to come back and run this place."

She stilled. "What?"

"Your dad mentioned they were thinking about selling when I called to make my reservation. He said you weren't interested in continuing in the hospitality business."

"He mentioned selling to you? Seriously?" She knew they'd been talking about it, but she hadn't realized until right this very minute that they were seriously ready to leave. Funny, Sunny thought. Before she'd come back to step in the idea of them selling the place had seemed like the best plan, but now... Oh, hell, now she didn't know how she felt. The idea of another owner, another family here...

It was Finn's turn to pause and he regarded her steadily. She resisted the urge to squirm beneath that direct scrutiny. "Was he not supposed to?"

She gave her head a small shake. "No, it's just that he must finally be coming around. They've been talking about it for months, but have very specific ideas about the buyer. I wonder if they've talked to a Realtor," Sunny mused aloud, a strange sense of panic in her chest. It was ridiculous. She didn't want this place; in fact, she had built her own life away from it. Her parents were ready—quite rightfully—to retire. And yet... She knew they hadn't talked to

Heath about it, though. Heath had certainly brought it up to her parents often enough. His eagerness had annoyed her father and frankly, neither one of her parents had been too keen on him.

"What do you mean exactly by 'specific ideas'?" Finn asked.

Sunny looked down the row of rooms, saw families sitting outside, much as they were, enjoying the cooler dusk temperatures. The scent of hamburgers on the grill flavored the air and the hum of an ice cream maker sounded somewhere close by. The Sandpiper was cozy, intimate and, because her parents had always been concerned with making sure the families who stayed here would come back, affordable.

She released a small sigh and her rueful gaze tangled with his. "They don't want it to change," Sunny confided. "The land the Sandpiper is sitting on is worth more than the business. When they put it on the market, developers are going to be circling like sharks. Mom and Dad are going to insist on a buyer who won't raze the place, but will continue to run it the way that they have, to preserve the family-friendly laid-back feel of the place. And then there's Tug, of course." She jerked her head toward the last unit.

Finn blinked and his head swiveled in the direction she'd indicated. "He's still here?"

"Yes," she said. "He's retired, though. Mom and Dad gave him Number Fifteen."

He sipped his whiskey. "That was generous."

"True," she agreed. "But he earned it."

Finn seemed to be mulling that over. He stared thoughtfully down at his Jack, swirling the remainder in the bottom of the glass. "It would be a shame for it to change," he said. "Some of my very best memories are of this place. That's why I came back."

There was an odd undercurrent in that statement, Sunny thought, giving him a closer look.

Feeling her scrutiny, he glanced up at her. "And if they can't find the right buyer? What do you think will happen then?"

"They'll stay. They'll have to hire help—much as he'd never admit it, Dad's getting too old to handle the bigger repairs—which will mean raising the rates, but it can't be helped." Feeling unreasonably defensive, Sunny shot him a look. "I bet you think I'm being incredibly unreasonable and selfish, don't you?"

His eyes widened in surprise. "Why the hell would I?"

"Because I don't want to stay here. Because I like my life the way it is. Because I spent the bulk of my childhood as an unpaid maid, babysitter and gopher." Feeling unaccountably antsy, she handed him her glass. "Top me off, would you?"

Finn chuckled, but obliged. "I don't think you're being selfish at all, Sunny," he told her. "It's not selfish to want to blaze your own trail. This—" he gestured to the inn "—is the life *they* chose. You are free to choose, as well." He relaxed more fully into his seat, impossibly taking up more room and his leg brushed hers, the innocent contact making her melt inside. "It would be unreasonable for anyone to think otherwise."

She'd need to hear that more than she realized, Sunny thought. Heath had certainly had a different take on the idea, that was for sure. He'd wanted her to "claim her rightful inheritance" and had told her that she'd be a fool not to do so. That she'd worked her butt off here and she deserved it. Of course, given that he'd been telling people that they were engaged—her blood boiled anew—and had basically promised the property to this Mr. Henniger, she was hardly surprised that he would take that stance. *Asshole,* she thought now. The next time he called—and there would definitely be a next time, particularly after what had happened today—she was going to give him a dressing-down he was never going to forget.

Finn hesitated, then turned to face her. "Listen, Sunny, there's something I need to say."

Oh, shit. She'd hoped to avoid this, had hoped that he'd just leave it be. She had no desire to rehash the past and honestly didn't care to hear any excuses. It made her feel pathetic that she even cared. She should be over it. Over him. And yet seeing him again made it all come rushing back. The keen affection, the aching desire, the inability to look at anything but him. He'd been her world twelve years ago and she'd practically orbited around him. But then he'd left, leaving a black hole where her heart had been.

"No, you don't," Sunny told him, her voice too bright. She hated that, but couldn't seem to control it. The more nervous she became, the higher her voice climbed.

"Yes, I do," he insisted, leaning forward, an earnest expression on his too-dear, too-handsome face.

Her mouth went dry and her heart kicked into a faster rhythm. "It's water under the bridge, Finn."

"Maybe so," he admitted, his voice low. "But I still have to tell you that I'm sorry. I'm not going to offer an excuse, because I don't have one that justifies my behavior. But I do regret that I didn't keep my promise to you. I—I need you to know that."

It would have been so much better if he hadn't apologized, Sunny thought despairingly. She could have left tonight, fulfilling her obligatory "catching-up" session so as not to appear rude, and then avoided him for the rest of the week. It wouldn't have been easy, particularly where her libido was concerned, but she could have done it. The apology—which she *did* deserve—didn't wipe the slate clean, but it showed her another facet of his character. It would have been easier to ignore him if she knew he didn't have any regret.

She swallowed. "Thank you," she said, touched. Her voice shook. "I appreciate that."

Her cell phone went off, sending Bill Withers's soulful "Ain't No Sunshine" into the warm night air.

"I like your ring tone," Finn said, chuckling softly. "Ironic for a girl named Sunny."

She grunted. "It was better than Shelly or Sandy," she said, checking the display. Sunny frowned and sent the call to voice mail. She had every intention of blasting Heath with the brunt of her considerable anger, but she wasn't going to do it in front of Finn.

Naturally, his keen gaze missed nothing and she watched the curiosity form in his eyes. "Telemarketer?" he asked, his tone deceptively light.

The devil poked her with his pitchfork. "Worse. Ex-boyfriend." Damned Heath. Miserable rotten bastard. But as an exit, this worked beautifully. There, she thought with a tiny bit of smugness. Finn could stew on that for a while. And, from the slightly irritated look on his face, that's exactly what he was doing. She handed him her glass and stood, then gathered Atticus's things.

His brows winged up his forehead in surprise, transforming his expression into something less readable. Panic maybe? "You're leaving?"

She steeled herself against him, against the pull to stay, the raw need hammering in her veins. "It's been great talking to you, Finn, but I've got an early morning."

"I thought you might want to have dinner. I've got a couple of steaks marinating. I could toss them on the grill real quick."

That certainly sounded better than the ham sandwich she'd be eating tonight, but being here with him felt too familiar. Too many walks down memory lane would weaken her resolve and land her right back in his bed. With little to no effort, she knew, thanks to her own traitorous libido. Finn hadn't made the first pass—he didn't have to. She could feel the energy humming between them, the ever-present current of desire that was only going to strengthen according to the amount of time she spent with him.

He was leaving again—off to war this time—and though her sixteen-year-old heart had ultimately recovered, she wasn't sure her twenty-eight-year-old one would be able to muster the wherewithal to bounce back.

A flash of loneliness and panic raced across his face so fast she was inclined to believe she'd imagined it. That hint of vulnerability pricked at her heart. It wasn't an expression she'd never seen on Finn's face before and it didn't fit at all. He'd always been so confident, so self-assured. That was part of what had drawn her to him in the first place. Even when they were children he'd been fearless. He'd never dreamed that he *couldn't* do something. He'd been her rebel with a cause, she thought fondly, remembering.

What was Finn afraid of now? she wondered. What was it specifically that he was either avoiding or not willing to face? Had he become so accustomed to being busy and surrounded by people—she imagined there wasn't much privacy in the military—that he didn't know how to be alone? To be still? Her gaze slid over him once more and she repressed a shudder of pure desire.

"Did you bring a kite?" she asked suddenly. If she didn't make her exit scene now, she was going to be incapable of it.

His brow furrowed at the abrupt subject change. "No. I didn't think about it."

"You should get one. And some books," she added as she hurriedly descended the deck stairs to the boardwalk that connected the rooms.

He frowned. "Why?"

"Because you've forgotten how to be still," she called as she started off. She breathed a silent sigh of relief, resisting the urge to look back and see what he thought about that little insight.

Intuition told her he probably wasn't going to like it.

TUG TIMMONS TIED OFF the fly he'd been working on, then sat back and rolled his shoulders. It was hell getting old, he thought. Determined to be the eternal beach bum, he'd spent the better part of thirty years here on this piece of sand. Though he would never say that he'd wasted his life, he had to admit that he did have a few regrets. He'd never married, never had children.

Of course, he'd never wanted to do either of those things until Martha Ann Bradford turned up ten years ago and upended his world. He could remember it like it was yesterday. He'd been working on the pool pump, muttering and cussing under his breath when he'd heard her laugh.

That was all.

She'd laughed and it had been so intriguing, so delightful, so beautiful that he'd stopped what he was doing and looked up. A siren's song, he realized now. And then, of course, he was done for.

Martha Ann had sleek blond hair—the kind that

merely looked lighter as the gray came in—and it had been cut into a style that brushed the nape of her neck and hung in a wave around her face, curling along her jaw. She had intelligent bright blue eyes and a soft smile that made a man think she was always enjoying a private joke. She hadn't uttered a word, hadn't actually looked in his direction, but none of that had mattered. It was as if a lightning bolt had struck when he'd looked at her, and he'd wanted her to be his with every fiber of his being.

He'd wanted to hold her hand, to hear her laugh again. He'd wanted to mine her mind for her thoughts and figure out what made her tick. He'd wanted to make her breakfast and rub her shoulders and watch the sun go up and down with her. He'd wanted to show her his beach, walk along the hard-packed sand and tell her why every grain was so special.

He'd just wanted her…and she'd been taken.

Then. But not anymore.

Tug knew it was bad form to speak ill of the dead, but he'd never cared much for Martha Ann's husband. Still, considering he'd fallen in love with the man's wife, it wasn't likely he'd ever genuinely like the guy, anyway. In the ten years that they'd been coming here, Tug had never once heard Sheldon Bradford say a single complimentary thing to or about his wife. He'd treated her as if she'd been put on the earth to serve him and as though any good qualities she had were merely a reflection of his own influence in her life.

He'd been a self-important, condescending ass. Tug grinned to himself. Not that he had an opinion on the subject or anything.

When Martha Ann had arrived a couple of weeks ago without Sheldon in tow and had conveyed her newly widowed status, the joy that had bolted through Tug had just about sent him to his knees.

She was free. Finally.

And he fully intended to make her his.

Of course, that would be a lot easier if she'd agree to spend some time with him. But he hadn't waited ten years for her to give up just because she was a little resistant. He knew that she was interested, whether she'd admit it or not. She watched him when she thought he wasn't looking, and she was bad to fidget when he came around. He made her nervous.

That was a start.

4

HE'D FORGOTTEN HOW TO BE still? Finn thought. What the hell was she talking about? He'd been sitting here with her for the better part of an hour and hadn't moved off the deck. He'd had to fight the impulse to move closer to her, certainly, and had been silently congratulating himself on his restraint. But he could be still, dammit. He could. If he wanted to.

Though he'd like to blame his desire to be nearer to her on the monumental sexual attraction—which, unbelievably, had only worsened since the last time he'd seen her—he knew something else was at work here, as well. He was drawn to her, for lack of a better description. He had to physically fight the compulsion to lessen the distance between them all the time.

Furthermore, though he'd been continually distracted by her mouth—specifically the way it moved—and the tanned expanse of bare leg only inches from his own thigh, Finn had to admit that it had been a long time since he'd felt so settled in his own skin. She was a restful kind of company, his Sunny, and while he was getting the impression that she'd like to keep some distance between them... Finn had no intention of letting that happen.

The small noble part of his character knew he should respect her wishes—especially after what had happened last time—but the more substantial selfish part wanted to make her change her mind.

And the confident, observant part of him knew he could.

Because she was every bit as attracted to him as he was to her. *That* part of their relationship, despite time and his bad behavior, hadn't changed. He could read it in the slow curve of her lips, the lingering feel of her gaze as it slid over his body. She'd unwittingly moved closer, tilted her head in toward him, a soft hitch in her breathing. Little tells that signaled that her body was going through a similar meltdown of desire. Hell, he'd gone hard when she'd bent over to set the dog dish down, and he had been fighting the erection ever since.

He snorted. Didn't know how to be still, his ass. He could be still.

He purposely threw himself back into his chair,

then popped back up as another thought surfaced. A dark one.

Okay, so maybe he couldn't be still when he was thinking about the ex-boyfriend. If the guy was an ex, then why was he calling her? Had they just broken up? Had they been living together and he was merely calling to coordinate getting some of his stuff back? Or was he an unwilling ex? Finn wondered grimly. One who wanted her back?

Little red spots danced behind his lids at the thought and he suddenly felt as if he'd eaten something that hadn't agreed with him. His fingers tightened on the deck rail and he pried them loose to toss back the rest of his whiskey. It took a moment for him to label the emotion swirling in the pit of his stomach and when he did, shock momentarily jolted through him.

Jealousy? He was jealous? Of the ex-boyfriend of a former lover he hadn't seen in twelve years?

Nah, Finn told himself, shaking his head. He was not jealous. He couldn't be. Certainly he was fond of Sunny and she'd been the only girl he'd ever imagined a future with, the only one who'd ever scared the hell out of him, and he definitely wanted her with an intensity that bordered on manic, but…jealous? He wasn't that invested, he told himself. He was simply outraged on her behalf. He'd seen her frown when she'd checked the caller ID. Clearly the guy was bothering her.

He would make him stop.

Glad that he had a purpose, Finn easily hopped over the deck railing and made his way down to Sunny's house. He'd always loved that the main home was just separate from the rest of the inn. Close enough to still be a part of things, but detached for a bit of privacy. It was a two-story shingled cottage with a small widow's walk. For as long he could remember, the house had been painted a pale moss-green accented with white trim and shutters.

White and hot-pink oleander bloomed against the structure, splashes of happy color along the front. Two swings were at either end of the long front porch and a small table and chairs sat to the right of the front door, a comfy place to sit and take in the view. He'd seen Audie and Janine enjoy their morning coffee there many times.

Before he could stop and ask himself what the hell he was doing, he mounted the steps and rapped on her door.

From inside the house he heard an ominous growling bark and the telltale sound of toenails scrambling on a hardwood floor. Atticus skidded around the corner and hurtled toward the screen. He drew up short when he reached it, left a trail of spit against the door and then greeted Finn in the usual form—by farting.

Finn knew there was a doorbell outside the main office that would ring here at the house, alerting the Ledbetters that a guest needed assistance, so Sunny had to be wondering who was at her door.

She peered out into the hall from the kitchen and her eyes widened with something more than recognition when she saw him. Relief, maybe? She'd pulled her hair into a ponytail and donned a white sleeveless shirt and men's boxer shorts. The ex-boyfriend's? he wondered, gritting his teeth.

Her gaze turned wary. "Finn? Did you need something?"

Yes, he thought. *A lobotomy.* Because clearly he was losing his freakin' mind. Over the mere idea of an ex-boyfriend.

"I wondered if I could borrow a book," he said, improvising quickly. He patted himself on the back for sounding almost normal. Though he could presently chew nails into scrap metal, his voice sounded strangely calm.

She blinked, still startled at seeing him on her porch evidently. She unlatched the screen door. "Er, I'm not sure that I'm going to have anything that you would find of interest, but you're welcome to go through what I've still got here."

He stepped inside and took a moment to bend down and rub one of Atticus's velvety ears. "You're a decent guard dog, old boy, and the gas?" He gave a thumbs-up. "That's an excellent deterrent."

Sunny chuckled. "That's the only benefit to it, believe me." Her gaze slid to him. "So, a book? Right." She nodded once. "Follow me."

He sniffed the air and smelled something sweet. "Are you making cinnamon rolls?"

She shot him a look over her shoulder and smiled. "No, but Mom often makes them and the scent lingers."

Indeed. It was mouthwatering. "I'm not interrupting you, am I?" he asked as he trailed behind her to the stairs. Her heart-shaped rear end swung back and forth in a mesmerizing fashion that left him curiously light-headed. He grunted under his breath. Probably because most of his blood was rushing from one head to the other.

"Nothing that can't wait."

Was she being purposely vague to torment him? he wondered. Why couldn't she just say what she was doing? Better still, why in sweet hell did he think it was any of his business?

Though he'd been to her house many times, he'd only been in her bedroom a handful of them. She had the same white spindly furniture she'd had when she was a teenager. A colorful quilt covered her bed and half a dozen pillows littered the surface. Framed photos from her childhood hung on the walls, various trophies—mostly for softball—sat on her chest of drawers and a small pink jewelry box with a single ballerina that didn't twirl held a place of honor on her dresser.

She led him over to a bookcase and said, "Take your pick."

"I'm surprised your parents didn't turn your room into a bigger bathroom or a guest bedroom when you moved out," he remarked, looking at the titles. Romance, romance and more romance. He was beginning to see a theme here. "Mine sure didn't waste any time," Finn said, laughing softly.

"I don't know if you've noticed this or not, but my parents tend to resist change," she said, a droll smile in her voice. She stubbed her big toe into the carpet and shifted nervously. So she didn't like him in here, did she? Too close to the bed to suit her? His lips twisted with masculine satisfaction.

"Have you read all of these?" he asked, trying to keep the grin under control.

"Of course. Why else would I have them?"

He shot her a smile over his shoulder. "Do you have anything that doesn't have a man and woman embracing on the cover?"

With a put-upon sigh she shouldered him out of the way, squatted down and selected a book from the shelf, then handed it to him.

He glanced at the title and raised a skeptical brow. *"Harry Potter and the Sorcerer's Stone?* Are you serious? Isn't it a kid's book?"

She lifted her chin. "Read the first fifty pages. If you're not hooked, I'll—"

"Have dinner with me," he interjected before she could finish. He had to seize the opportunities when she presented them, after all. He was only here four more days, then it was back to his reality. Orphaned soldier, no home, no family. His chest tightened and a bizarre sort of panic punched him in the gut. He shook the unsettling sensation off. Geez, Lord. What the hell was wrong with him?

She grinned, recognizing the ploy for what it was. "I was going to say—"

But whatever she was going to say was interrupted by the ringing of her cell phone again. She made another ominous face, growled low in her throat and bolted downstairs. After a second's hesitation, Finn followed her.

She'd just looked at the display when he caught up with her in the kitchen. "Dammit," she muttered, obviously irritated. "I'm going to have to take this. Excuse me a minute."

She left him standing in the kitchen and walked into the dining room, presumably for some privacy. He noted sandwich fixings on the counter and tried not to be annoyed, then edged closer to the door so that he could listen to her. Yes, it was rude. Yes, his mother had taught him better. Yes, he was still going to do it.

He was curious, dammit. And if she was in some sort of trouble or needed assistance with anything, then he intended to help her.

"Listen, Heath," he heard her say through clenched teeth. "It's over, you understand? We're not dating anymore. Ever. Period. I don't want to see you anymore. I thought I made that clear. I—"

Masculine pleasure bloomed in his chest, pushing a smile across his lips.

"I'm sorry that you feel that way, but you are going to have to leave me alone. Stop calling me. Stop coming by my apartment. Stop dropping by my store. And for the love of all that's holy, don't ever tell another person that I'm your fiancée. Let it go," she said, her voice so hard it should have shattered Heath's balls. "If you don't, I'm going to have to contact the authorities."

An alarm sounded in the back of Finn's mind. If she was threatening to call the cops, in all likelihood she probably already should have. That's the way it usually worked.

He *was* going to have to make the jackass go away, Finn thought, familiar adrenaline—his fix—hitting his system.

A course of action quickly came to mind. Finn abruptly walked into the dining room and in loud, carrying tones said, "Baby, this massage oil is going to get cold if you don't come back to bed."

Sunny inhaled with shock, her eyes widened in horror and then narrowed into tiny little slits that were shooting a very convincing death ray at him.

Oh, hell, Finn thought. That didn't exactly look like gratitude to him.

"Who's that?" Heath demanded, his voice throbbing with anger. "You're seeing someone else? *Already?* I can't believe you, Sunny. I thought we had something special. I thought—"

"Whatever we had is *over,* Heath. For the last time, stop calling me." She abruptly closed the phone before he could say anything else and made a mental note to call her cell company and have his number blocked. She released a huge breath, hoping to ease a bit of the tension gathering rapidly in her shoulders.

It didn't work.

She glared at Finn. *"This massage oil is going to*

get cold?" she repeated, each word coming out more mangled than the last. "Have you lost your *freaking* mind?" she practically screamed at him. Anger had replaced the initial shock and she could literally feel the top of her head vibrating, ready to blow. "Where in the hell do you get off interfering in my personal business? What makes you think you have the right?" Her gaze narrowed. "I don't know what world you've been living in, Rambo, but that *wasn't* cool."

He retreated a step, and, though she imagined her vision was wobbly due to the fact she was literally quaking with irritation, she thought she saw his lips twitch. "Rambo?"

He *was* laughing at her, the wretch. "Finn, I am not amused."

He tried unsuccessfully to flatten his lips. "I can see that. I can't believe you s-stomped your f-foot. I've never seen a girl do that b-before." He didn't just laugh, he roared. She'd never wanted to whack another person more, Sunny realized.

She crossed her arms over her chest to keep from doing just that. "I did *not* stomp my foot." At least, she didn't think she had, though she supposed it was possible.

"You did," he wheezed, his big shoulders quaking. "God, that was priceless. The next time I need a laugh, I'm pulling that memory out."

She flushed, mortified, then bared her teeth in a smile. "Not if I knock your head off your shoulders first."

He stilled and studied her thoughtfully for a moment. His eyes widened in surprise. "You're really pissed."

"You think?" she asked sarcastically. "You should probably brush up on those deductive reasoning skills while you're here. Maybe work a few crosswords or something."

"I was only trying to help, Sunny. I—"

She almost stomped her foot again, but resisted the impulse and tossed her cell phone into the nearest chair instead. "I didn't ask for your help, Finn."

He lifted his chin and something shifted in his gaze. Grew harder and more intuitive. "Maybe not, but you need it."

A finger of unease nudged her middle. "What makes you say that?"

"Those deductive reasoning skills you seem to think I need to work on," he said, his lips curving into a grim smile. That barb had struck a nerve. "He phoned while you were down at my place and you ignored the call. Less than an hour later, he's made contact again and, from the sounds of your end of the conversation, it's been going on for a while."

"It's rude to eavesdrop," she muttered, plopping down on the sofa with a dejected thump.

He sat down next to her, entirely too close for comfort. A current of heat snaked through her, irritating her all the more. She was too aware of him for comfort, too sensitive to every breath that went in and out of his lungs, the fine hair on his arms brushing hers. "I would have heard you even if I hadn't been trying."

Spent, she managed a weak laugh. "You're not even going to try to deny it, are you?"

She felt him shrug and knew that he had moved closer. Again. She smothered an inevitable sigh. "I don't see the point. Besides, you baited me with the ex-boyfriend comment before you left."

She feigned offense. "I didn't bait you!"

He chuckled. "Liar."

Sunny harrumphed and rolled her eyes. "Being a soldier has obviously made you paranoid."

"Being a soldier has made me extremely observant. I saw that smug little smile when you turned to leave."

Damn. And she thought she'd been so cool. "You do get regular physical exams in the army, right? I think you might need to get your eyes checked."

"And I think you need a restraining order. Heath

doesn't sound like the kind of guy who's going to give up."

She grimly suspected he was right, but didn't want to admit it to him. "Oh, I'm sure he'll stop now that he knows that I'm getting rubbed down with heated massage oil by another guy," she said, purposely injecting a huge load of sarcasm into her voice. "I still can't believe you said that. Moron," she complained.

A sexy chuckle rumbled up Finn's throat. "I'm sure he's only sorry that he didn't think of it first."

She turned to look at him. "And what makes you think he didn't?"

A comical amount of confidence faded from his smile. "Did he?"

She turned away and sniffed primly. "I don't see where that's any of your business."

Finn sighed happily, the self-assured smile back on his face. "That's a no then."

"Sandwalwood is my favorite," Sunny said thoughtfully. "It's warm with a touch of spice and a hint of rose, the perfect combination of sensual and romantic. I also like lemon verbena. So…invigorating." She lingered purposely over that last word and gave a delicate little shudder. She popped up from the couch. "So, you've got your book?"

He blinked stupidly and his beautiful mouth had gone a bit slack. "Come again?"

"Your book," she reminded slowly. "The one you came over here for."

Finn didn't stand. "Oh, yeah."

"Did you leave it upstairs?"

His brooding gaze found hers. "I left it in the kitchen. I'll get it when I leave."

Meaning he wasn't ready to leave yet, despite her quite obvious hint. She exhaled a slow breath. "Finn—"

"How long has this been going on? How long did you and this Heath guy date? How long since you dumped him?"

She shook her head and looked heavenward for divine assistance. How was she supposed to avoid Finn if he barged into her space? How was she supposed to keep from sitting in his lap and kissing his neck and slipping her hands all over his body if he wouldn't leave her alone? "You have no concept of personal boundaries, do you?"

His unwavering stare was dead-serious and unnerving. She felt herself flush. "Your safety is very personal to me."

She'd have to be made of stone not to appreciate his concern and sincerity. She found herself reluctantly softening toward him. "Finn, I'm perfectly safe."

"I don't think you are. How long has he been harassing you?"

"Several weeks," she admitted. She moved to the mantel and adjusted a photograph. "He just doesn't want to accept that I've broken things off." She couldn't tell him the rest. It was too embarrassing.

"How long did you see him?"

Since he wasn't going to leave, she might as well sit back down, Sunny thought, but took a chair instead of joining him on the couch. "A couple of months."

"Intimate?"

Beating that horse to death, wasn't he? she thought, inwardly pleased. "None of your business."

The edge of his mouth tilted. "It could be important."

"I doubt it."

He grimaced. "Why did you break up?"

"Because I knew it was a dead-end relationship and I don't like to waste my time," she said.

That wasn't the only reason, of course, but there was no way in hell she was telling him that Heath had been telling other developers that once the Sandpiper was hers, it was as good as his. It was just too damned galling to admit. She was eternally thankful that she hadn't slept with him.

Sunny had a healthy libido and had had several lovers over the years—some more serious than others—but she was especially selective when deciding who she shared her body with. There was a level of trust that had to be met first and, with Heath, they never gotten to that point. He'd been attentive, courteous and said all the right things…but something inside of her simply hadn't been able to make that leap.

"And how long since you ended it?"

"Three weeks ago."

Finn's expression blackened. "So, long enough for him to recognize that it's a lost cause." His gaze slid to hers. "Something's not right, Sunny. Any man with a grain of self-respect would have backed off by now. He's harassing you and, from the sounds of it, with increasing frequency. You need to report him, get a restraining order."

She'd resisted that idea because she didn't want to overreact, but hearing Finn say it somehow made the idea more credible. And after Mr. Henniger's appearance today, she had to admit that Heath was becoming increasingly erratic and irrational.

She released a shaky breath. "Okay."

He nodded once, seemingly pleased and settled more firmly against her couch. "In the meantime, I'm staying here."

5

FINN KNEW THE MINUTE the words left his mouth that she was going to vehemently resist and he was right. Sunny gasped like a dying fish, then bolted up from her chair. A long curl escaped her ponytail and her cheeks pinkened.

"You are not," she said, a hint of hysteria and desperation in the protest.

He shrugged lazily, confident that this was the right move. "It only makes sense."

And it did.

This Heath guy was definitely a threat and, though Finn had only been trying to help with his massage-oil comment, he grimly suspected that it might have actually made things worse. He'd thought that if Heath had caught the scent of another guy around Sunny, he'd back off and give up the idea of a reconciliation. But he wasn't dealing with the average guy here and had a hunch that his stunt had only painted a bigger target on Sunny's back.

That was *his* fault and he'd be damned if he'd sit idly by and do nothing.

And if he'd learned anything today, it was that he didn't seem to be capable of *doing nothing*.

Sunny looked away, seemingly trying to figure out a way to frame a reply. She looked miserable and desperate and just a smidge hysterical. "Listen, Finn, it's not that I don't appreciate the offer, but it really isn't necessary. I've got Atticus—" she jerked her head in the dog's direction "—and Heath doesn't even know I'm here. I'm perfectly safe."

He shook his head. "All the same, I'd feel better—"

"Well, I wouldn't," she interjected, the wild look back in her eyes. Her pulse fluttered rapidly at the base of her throat, and suddenly her panicked reluctance made sense. He'd already noted that she was still attracted to him, that the desire hammering away at him was taking a mallet to her, as well. Too much temptation then? he wondered. Didn't trust herself around him?

Finn felt a slow-dawning smile drift across his lips. It was all he could do not to preen. "Why wouldn't you? It's not like you don't know me."

Her own gaze grew mistrustful as she noted his grin. "I haven't seen you in *twelve* years, Finn. I knew the boy. The man is still a mystery."

"I'm the same guy," he told her.

She lifted her chin. "Then that's disappointing. I was hoping you'd matured a bit."

That dart penetrated because it was accurate and well-deserved. He swallowed. Well, while they were being truthful… He laughed softly and shook his head. "I know why you don't want me to stay."

"Yes, because I just told you," she bit out, evidently irritated by the innuendo in his tone.

A bark of laughter erupted from his throat. "That's not why."

She blinked in exaggerated confusion. "It's not? Oh, gee, Finn. Then why don't you tell me?"

"Because you want me," he told her. "And if I'm here with you, then I'm too close."

She did the guppy face again and the whites of her eyes kept getting bigger and bigger. "You— I—" She emitted a long, frustrated growl, then pointed to the door. "Out!"

"Sunny—"

She started toward him and picked up the closest thing at hand, a heavy ceramic vase, and drew her arm back.

Startled, he jumped up. "I'm going," he said before she could hurl it at him.

"Not fast enough," she said through gritted teeth.

He swung through the kitchen and snagged his book, then headed for the back door. "Sunny, listen to me. I really think that you need a guy around. I don't think—"

She laughed without humor. "No, you don't, but that still doesn't keep your mouth from working, does it?" She opened the door and shoved him through it, staggering a bit as she did so. "This is not your problem, Finn. You're on vacation. Deal with it."

She abruptly slammed the door.

She was wrong—this *was* his problem.

And she might have gotten mad, considered attacking him and kicked him out of her house because he'd told her that he knew that she wanted him…but not once had she denied it.

This battle was far from over, but if there was ever a time to retreat, this was it. Finn shoved his hands into his pockets and, whistling tunelessly, strolled over to the porch swing and took up his post.

SHE LOOKED LIKE DEATH WARMED over, Sunny thought as she met her reflection in the mirror the next morning. The bags under her eyes had their own set of luggage and her head ached from lack of sleep.

Ugh.

Adding another black mark next to Finn's name, she stepped into the shower, hoping to wash some of the irritation away. She'd forgotten just how easily he'd always been able to yank her chain. Her feelings where he was concerned had never been mediocre and the reactions he inspired in her only followed suit.

Of course, it didn't help matters that he was right.

And, more gallingly, that he knew it.

She groaned aloud and pushed her face beneath the spray.

When he'd announced that he was going to stay with her, Sunny had gone into full-blown panic mode. She'd had a hard enough time leaving him when he'd asked her to stay for dinner. In fact, she'd actually felt guilty about it. But she'd left because every second that she spent with him only intensified the attraction. Only made her more hammeringly aware of the exact curve of his smile, his sleepy heavy-lidded gaze, the mesmerizing shape of his hands—big and competent—and how they would feel sliding up her skin.

To be perfectly honest, Sunny wanted him to want

her. Wanted him to burn and ache for her, to make him crazy with desire.

But she wanted to resist him.

The fly in the ointment? She wasn't altogether certain that she *could* resist him. That's why she'd freaked. That's why she'd lost any resemblance to a rational human being when he'd confronted her with the mortifying truth and, like a crazed harpy, had rushed him to the door.

She did want him. Still.

Against all reason and better judgment. It didn't matter that he'd broken her heart, that he'd left her once without so much as a postcard later. It didn't matter that he was leaving again. It only mattered that he was here now, however fleetingly, and that Finn O'Conner still had the ability to melt her heart.

Though she knew she was fighting a losing battle, Sunny nevertheless would continue to fight. She couldn't afford not to. He'd wounded her before, she knew, but something told her that this time around when he left, she'd be obliterated. The life that she'd managed to carve out for herself would lose its luster when he left, and she'd never be able to find her happy place again, because he wouldn't be in it.

Not no, but, hell, no.

Furthermore, she'd taken a cheap shot when she'd said she didn't know him. That she'd known the boy and not the man. True, she hadn't seen him in the last twelve years and there were many things that had happened to him during that time that were a mystery to her…but she did *know* him.

Her Finn was there, more mature, of course, but she still recognized him. He was the merciful guy who gave a pass to the young teenager who'd accidentally killed his parents; he was the sentimental guy who tucked Smarties into his father's pocket at the funeral. He was the humble guy who tendered an apology more than a decade late, just because it was the right thing to do. She swallowed.

He was still her Finn…and that made him all the more lethal.

Sunny rinsed her hair, then shut the water off and reached for her towel. Furthermore, much as she'd like to think that he simply wanted to stay with her to charm his way back into her bed—and she wasn't stupid enough to think he wouldn't try—Sunny believed that he was genuinely worried about her safety. She'd seen the look on his face, the anger and concern when she'd finally admitted how long Heath had been bothering her. And he was right. It was past time for Heath to know that any chance of getting back together was a lost cause. Hadn't she suspected something was off? Hadn't there been a niggle of unease?

Hadn't she noted the panicked note in Heath's voice? The hint of hysteria lurking in his tone?

Clint, their part-time summer help—big on muscle, short on common sense—would be in today at ten and she had every intention of going down to the police department and seeing precisely what she needed to do to make Heath leave her alone. Having Mr. Henniger show up yesterday had really clued her in to how out of touch with reality Heath was.

To ease some of Finn's anxiety, she'd let him know, Sunny decided. And this way, she avoided becoming a project, because she knew damned well he was looking for one. He didn't have a clue how to simply enjoy the moment anymore, to appreciate a sunset or the feel of sand beneath his feet. What was he avoiding? Sunny wondered. What thoughts crept in during the ensuing quiet that he didn't want to deal with? Why didn't he want to be still? Was it the war? The death of his parents? Probably a combination of both, she decided, which would make anyone not want to be in their own head.

But he was going to have to be, Sunny decided, because, as much as she'd like to help him, she didn't think she could risk her own sanity in the process. She was happy, dammit, and wanted to stay that way. Her good life wouldn't be so good anymore if she let him in, if she let him get too close. All the things that she'd told herself that she could do without—a lover, a family of her own—she'd start wanting again, and the contented world she'd built would crumble around her in ruins.

She couldn't let that happen.

Sunny shuffled through her bag until she found something to wear, then made quick work of drying her hair. When she ended up with more frizz than curls, she resignedly pulled it into a ponytail. Her hair had a mind of its own and she didn't know from one day to the next how it was going to look. She'd tried every styling product known to man and nothing had ever made a whit of difference. A couple of swipes of the mascara wand, a bit of blush and lip gloss and she was good to go.

Though her mother used to make a variety of breakfast foods every morning for their guests and put them out in the office, they'd stopped doing that a couple of years ago and instead had an assorted mixture of donuts and danishes delivered from a local bakery. For an extra buck, they'd been bringing a pot of spiced tea, as well. Sunny checked her watch, winced, then quickly put Atticus on the leash and grabbed his bowl and a chew toy. He'd been standing at the back door for the past fifteen minutes and she assumed a potty break was in order.

She'd taken one step onto the porch when she

realized there'd been a different reason the dog had been parked in front of the exit.

She let out a mighty breath.

Finn had been semireclined on the porch swing, but had moved into an upright position when she'd opened the door.

"Morning, sunshine," he said, his voice rusty, as though him being on her porch at 6:00 a.m. was a normal occurrence. His clothes were wrinkled, his hair mussed. Impossibly, he looked even better than he had last night.

She closed her eyes tightly, then opened them again. Nope. He was still there. *Damn.* She hung her head and released a long, dredged-from-the-bottom-of-her-soul sigh. Could she have actually forgotten how stubborn he'd always been?

"Please do not tell me that you've been out here all night."

He stood and stretched, making his muscles bunch and move in ways that made her appreciate the male anatomy. And more specifically, his. "Okay, I won't tell you."

"Did you stay out here all night?" she demanded.

"It's too early in the morning for you to start playing mind games with me, Sunny. I thought you just said you didn't want me to tell you."

"Finn!" she cried, whimpering with frustration. "I told you to go home."

"No, you just kicked me out of the house," he corrected. "The next time you run me off, you're going to have to be more specific." He rubbed his eyes tiredly. "I need coffee."

She needed something stronger, but it was too early to drink. "I can't believe you spent the night on the damned porch swing. Why didn't you go back to your room?"

"We've been over that, remember? You don't want me in the house? That's cool. I'm used to being outside."

She could quite cheerfully throttle him, Sunny thought, descending the stairs. Atticus led her over to a patch of sea oats and hiked his leg, then steered her toward the office. She could feel Finn behind her, trailing along in her wake. "So what? You're just going to follow me around all day?"

"No, there are going to be times when you're going to have to follow me. For instance, I need to shower and change clothes. Since I'm not going to be able to do that at your house, then you'll need to wait on me in my room." He smiled at her. "I'll hurry."

She unlocked the office door and pushed inside, feeling inevitability closing in on her from all sides. Her stomach tightened, an indistinguishable cramp of want and irritation. He'd spent the night on her porch, she thought, softening unwillingly, simply because he wanted to protect her, to keep her safe. Had any man ever done anything for her that could come close to a comparison? No. Still...

"Finn, for the last time, this isn't necessary. I'm going today to get a restraining order. I don't need a bodyguard." Though if she was going to have a bodyguard, a girl could do a helluva lot worse than Finn O'Conner. Geez Lord, he was a beautiful man. Tall and lean, with muscles on muscles and skin that begged for her touch. She smothered another whimper and dragged her gaze away from his distracting mouth. It was a little full for a man, but unbelievably sexy all the same. She wanted to feel it beneath her own lips and gliding along her jaw, feeding at her breasts. Warmth pooled in her center, making her shift.

His gaze narrowed at something over her shoulder. "What does Heath look like?"

"Like a soap-opera star. Blond hair, blue eyes, trendy dresser." She frowned. "Why?"

His brow formed a menacing line and a skitter of unease slid down her spine. "Because a guy matching that description is staring at us through the window."

Sunny gasped and whirled. *Damn.*

6

FINN LOCKED EYES WITH the stranger who he suspected was Sunny's ex and felt the hair on the back of his neck rise. White-hot anger bolted through him, tripping some sort of trigger he'd never disengaged before. *This* was the man who was harassing Sunny. *This* was the man who wouldn't take no for an answer. *This* was the man who she may or may not have slept with.

Sunny's jaw dropped and some of the color leached from her face. "I can't believe this," she said faintly. "What have I done to deserve this?" A thundercloud of irritation worked its way across her previously smooth brow and she started forward.

He caught her arm. "Oh, no," he said, his voice hardening. "I've got this."

"I can fight my own battles, Finn," she all but growled.

"But that's the beauty of it." He flashed her a smile devoid of humor. "You don't have to." He strode forward and opened the door just as Heath was reaching for the handle, blocking him from entering. "Listen, buddy, you and I need to have a little talk."

Heath merely grimaced and made the mistake of trying to go around Finn. "Sunny, I—"

Finn grabbed the back of Heath's neck and squeezed, the way you would control a recalcitrant puppy, then steered him farther away from the office. Heath yelped with pain and tried to wriggle out of Finn's grip. "Get your hands off me! Who the hell do you think you are?"

Why was everyone asking him that? Finn wondered. He gave Heath a harder than necessary shove into the porch railing to make sure he had his full attention. "I'm a friend of Sunny's and I'm here to convey a message." He lowered his voice to a lethal level and speared the man with a straight look. "Leave her alone. Do not ever contact her again. *Ever.* Do you understand?"

Heath's mouth formed a condescending sneer and he made the unfortunate decision to dismiss Finn's threat. "The only thing I understand is that I don't take orders from you. I—"

"Wrong answer." Finn slammed his fist into Heath's jaw and sent him flying backward over the railing. Damn, that felt good. Not as good as the sex he'd like to have with Sunny, but there was a lot to be said for expending some energy this way, too.

Horrified, Sunny rushed outside. "Finn, don't!"

Finn ignored her, easily leaping over the railing and crossing his arms over his chest. "Let's try this again," he said. "Leave. Sunny. Alone." He enunciated each word plainly and succinctly, as though he were speaking to someone of limited intelligence. Which he was. "She does not want to see you ever again. Do you understand?"

Heath spat a wad of blood from his mouth and looked past him. "Sunny?"

"Oh, for heaven's sake," she wailed. "Go, Heath! It's over."

Finn reached down and dragged Heath to his feet. "Come on, Heath. I'll help you to your car," he growled, giving him a shake for good measure.

"I don't want your help. Get your hands off me," Heath said again, struggling to get out of Finn's grip. He'd be lucky if Heath didn't file assault charges against him, Finn thought, but decided it didn't matter. Hitting him had been worth it.

"Which one is yours?"

"The Lexus."

Of course, Finn thought. The guy was wearing a designer shirt, penny loafers and more jewelry than his great-aunt Marge. He was slicker than goose shit and Finn was having a very hard time figuring out just what in the hell Sunny had seen in him in the first place.

He opened the car door and shoved Heath inside. "Have some self-respect, man. She doesn't want you."

Heath looked as though he was considering running Finn over with his car, but ultimately he sped out of the lot. He did not look like a man who was going to give up just because Finn had nailed him in the jaw and sent his ass sprawling into the sand.

When Finn came back around the building, Sunny was waiting for him.

"You dated a guy who wears a pinky ring? Seriously, Sunny?"

She flushed. "Say what you want, but he's handsome."

For whatever reason, that absolutely infuriated him. "He's slick. And he's a wuss. The pansy-ass never even tried to hit me back. What kind of guy takes a punch and doesn't retaliate?"

"Not everyone can be a badass, Finn," she said with a beleaguered eye-roll. She turned and walked back into the office.

Something warm settled in his chest and he smiled. "You think I'm a badass?" he asked, following her.

She snorted. "Don't play coy. You know you're a badass."

He shrugged. "I'm not afraid to throw a punch if I think it's warranted, and I'll come out swinging if I'm backed into a corner. If that makes me a badass, then I guess I am." He paused. "He's not going to back off."

She looked up at him. "Even after what just happened?"

Finn shook his head. "I don't think so. He looked thwarted when he left, but not defeated."

She swore, a line he longed to smooth furrowing her brow. "So you still think I need the restraining order?"

"Definitely." There was something more at play here, something else Heath was after. The eternal question, of course, was what?

Sunny bit her bottom lip and another anxious line wormed across her forehead. The expression bothered him, made him want to chase Heath down and pummel him again.

Finn put a finger under her chin and lifted her face. "Hey, no worries, okay? I've got this." He smiled down at her. "I'll stay on your porch." He jerked his head toward Atticus. "He's not your only guard dog."

"I wonder how long he's been sitting out in the parking lot," she said.

"Long enough for the dew to collect on the hood of his car."

Her stomach rolled. "Do you think he came near the house?"

"I didn't hear him if he did."

"You wouldn't. The ocean," she reminded him.

It had been pretty loud, certainly noisy enough that he could have missed hearing Heath, much as he hated to admit it. Nevertheless, he shuddered to think what might have happened had he *not* been on her porch. Finn would rather go toe to toe with another badass any day than deal with a coward. A badass wasn't afraid to rumble and a guy knew what to expect. But a coward… Cowards were sneaky and unpredictable.

"Did Atticus notice anything?"

"Nothing, and you were on the porch all night." She glared at the dog. "You've got to do better," she scolded.

Predictably, Atticus farted in response to the criticism.

It was possible that Heath had seen him on the porch—he would have approached the house from that direction—and backtracked. After a moment, Finn said as much. "I'll install some motion-sensor lights," he told her. "Your parents need them anyway. It's a good precautionary measure. Anything that gets close enough to set them off near the porch needs to be illuminated, right?"

She nodded. "Thanks, Finn."

He grinned, glad that she seemed to be rallying. "Anytime. So do you need to put a sign on the door or what?"

"What do you mean?"

"The restraining order. We need to go down to the police station."

"I can't leave until Clint gets here."

Another man? Just how many guys were orbiting through her life? he wondered irritably. "Who's Clint?"

"Our part-time help. He comes in during the summer on Tuesdays and Thursdays." She glanced at the clock on the wall. "He'll be here at ten."

Finn nodded once. "We'll go then. What exactly do you do now?"

"Set breakfast out," she said. "It should be here soon. I'll check the weather for the day and post it on the door. Do a sweep of the grounds, pick up any stray trash. I've got people in Number Two and Number Five who are leaving today, so those rooms will have to be cleaned and ready by three because they're booked again."

"I'll help you."

She winced regretfully. "Finn, you're on vacation, you've had no sleep. You do not have to help me. Heath is gone. I seriously doubt he's going to come right back here. Go beach it today. Read your book or—"

"I've already read it," he told her. Her startled look was especially gratifying. "Would you happen to have *The Chamber of Secrets?*"

"You've already read it?" she repeated skeptically.

"I have," he confirmed with a nod. "Last night. You were right. I *did* like it." He made a moue of regret. "Pity, too. I almost wish I hadn't so I could get that dinner you were going to owe me."

She laughed, the sound vibrating something deep inside of him. "If you read that book from cover to cover last night, then I'll make you dinner."

"Do you want to quiz me?"

She was looking at him with the strangest expression, Finn thought. A mixture of helplessness and affection and something else, something he couldn't readily identify. It made his guts tingle and shake.

Still smiling, she shook her head. "I'll take your word for it."

"If you'll do that from now on, we'll argue a lot less."

She stilled, grew more serious. "Finn, thank you. For keeping watch," she clarified. "I have to admit I'm a little spooked."

He was, too, but for an entirely different reason. He felt it again, that tug behind his navel that was drawing him closer and closer to her. A sense of dawning inevitability, of Fate making a play. It was the same sensation that had sent him running last time.

He would not run again.

Unwittingly, he lessened the distance between them, reached up and ran the pad of his thumb over her lower lip. She gasped and her gaze darted up to his. She had the prettiest green eyes, Finn thought, and a lone freckle on her lid. Odd that he should find that so compelling. Adorable even. He brushed his lips over hers once, twice. She tasted like minty toothpaste and cherries, Finn noted vaguely, and the soft sigh that she finally breathed into his mouth as she melted against him held the sweetest flavor of all.

Victory.

SHE WISHED SHE HADN'T SEEN that, Sunny thought, that flash of something sweet and funny and, God help her, *tender* in his gaze. She'd been having a hard enough time dealing with the heat, those char-ring glances that made her belly knot up and her nipples tingle. The desire she could have potential-ly—though doubtfully—ignored for a little while longer, anyway.

But that other look? Whatever was left of her will simply crumbled away, weakening her body in the process. She sagged against him and the feel of his big, hard body next to hers, the slide of that incredibly carnal mouth over her lips made her want to weep with joy.

She slid her hands up over his arms, savoring mus-cle and sleek skin and he deepened the kiss with a groan. His tongue tangled around hers, a mindless seek-and-retreat as he made love to her mouth.

No two ways about it, Finn O'Conner was a damned fine kisser.

Nothing ruined a kiss faster than too much spit or concrete lips or what she liked to call the Dale Earnhardt, the fast kisser bent on lapping her mouth like the Talledega Speedway, then moving on to other things.

If a guy couldn't master the basics, then chances were he was a lousy lover. Sunny didn't have sex often enough to waste her time with someone who didn't know what the hell they were doing, so a bad first kiss was always a deal-breaker.

Finn, however, kept the moisture at that elusive level between too wet and too dry; his lips were masterful, molding *around* hers rather than *against* them, and he'd set the speed dial on Cruise, as though he would be content to kiss her all day long and never tire of it. His hands roamed her body, first bracketing her face, then trailing down over her shoulders and back, his thumbs along her spine.

Sunny slid her hands up and over his neck, into his hair, and the short locks felt smooth against her palm. The low hum of desire that had been thrumming in her womb had expanded to her sex and she could feel a resulting throb with every hurried beat of her heart. The achy heaviness of need weighted her breasts and she felt her nipples pearl behind her bra.

Finn's hands slowly shaped her rump and he gave a low growl of approval in her mouth as he gently squeezed. She felt the long, hard length of him nudge her belly and a thrill of feminine satisfaction whipped through her. Her sex wept, readying for him, and she squirmed against him. Finn lifted her bottom and set her on the desk behind the counter, then sidled in between her legs, applying the pressure she so desperately craved between her thighs.

It was her turn to groan and she felt him smile against her lips.

He rocked forward, snatching the breath from her lungs in a loud gasp that was almost embarrassing. She could feel the tension coiled in his body, the purely masculine energy that was so potent it was practically intoxicating. She felt drugged, primed, desperate.

From a mere kiss.

She was doomed.

"When do you have to fix breakfast?" he murmured against her mouth.

Breakfast? she wondered, trying to make sense of the word. *Breakfast!* Oh, hell. She froze and glanced at the clock. "Shirley will be here with it in a few minutes."

"No problem," he said, dragging her closer to him and flexing determinedly against her. "I only need one."

"Finn—"

He killed her protest with a nuzzle of his nose along her throat and did something with his hips that perfectly aligned their bodies to where he hit her sweet spot. She inhaled sharply and he chose that moment to move her shirt aside and pull her nipple into his mouth through her lacy bra.

The feeling was exquisite, his hot mouth, the damp fabric, the perfect tug as he suckled her. He flexed again, then increased the tempo, bumping her clit with every deliberate thrust. Each hit pushed her further and further to the edge, closer and closer to release. Sunny clamped her feminine muscles, sank her teeth into her bottom lip and listened as her breath ran away from her.

"Don't make me a liar," he murmured, then began to count down. "Five."

Harder.

"Four."

Faster.

"Three."

He licked her throat.

"Two."

He dragged her nipple back into his mouth, sucking deep, and pressed himself more firmly against her.

"One," he breathed, a smile in his voice, as she shattered.

Little colored dots floated behind her closed lids, her sex spasmed over and over, each contraction more powerful than the last, and her limbs felt as though her bones had turned to rubber. Weighted, sated and limp. He didn't move, but stayed against her until every bit of release had pulsed out of her body.

Still breathing heavily, Sunny dropped her head against his chest.

There was no way in hell he was sleeping on her porch after that.

"You can have the guest bedroom," she said.

She felt his chuckle vibrate against her forehead. "You're letting me into the house? That was the key? An orgasm?" He sighed dramatically. "Damn, I wish I'd known that last night." He drew back and looked down at her, a wicked gleam in his eye. "What's it going to take to upgrade from the guest bedroom to yours?"

"A voodoo priestess and a live chicken," Sunny deadpanned because she desperately needed to lighten the moment.

Finn's eyes widened, then deep, rumbling laughter bubbled up his throat. She loved the way he laughed. It was honest and unrestrained, infectious, she realized as she began to chuckle along with him.

She might as well laugh now. No doubt she'd be crying later.

Eyes twinkling with latent humor, Finn merely looked at her and shook his head. "You have a very frightening imagination, you know that?"

She shrugged helplessly. "It entertains me."

"I can see where it would."

What was it going to take for him to upgrade from the guest bedroom to hers? Sunny thought as she stared up at Finn, a sense of inevitability, resignation and anticipation settling around her. She sighed softly.

Very, very damned little, she feared.

7

"MORNING, MARTHA ANN."

Though she knew that she should be expecting it—Tug had greeted her in the exact same way every morning for the past two weeks—she was always a little surprised when he continued to make the effort. Pleasantly so, she would admit.

"Morning, Tug," she responded with a put-upon sigh, feeling a flush of unwanted pleasure move through her chest.

His gaze slid over her body, lingering on her breasts. Impossibly, her nipples tingled and she felt twin flags of color rise on her cheeks. "Still working on your tan, I see."

She resisted the urge to fan herself. Goodness, what was wrong with her? "It's typically what one does when one vacations at the beach."

"How much longer are you going to be here,

Martha Ann? I don't remember you and Sheldon ever staying more than a week at a time."

That's because Sheldon had had fair skin, burned easily and was too vain to use sunblock because he thought it wasn't masculine. He'd invariably burn and then be ready to go long before their vacation was supposed to be over. It had been damned annoying.

"I'm here for another week," she finally answered. And she was considering staying longer, if her room wasn't booked. Her children were grown, her grand-kids in college. She talked to them every few days, but there was nothing pressing for her to go back to, nothing on her calendar that couldn't wait. Why shouldn't she enjoy herself? Martha Ann thought. Why should she rush back to…nothing.

His smile widened, as though he was genuinely pleased. "I'm glad to hear it. The beach is always nicer when there's a pretty woman on it."

She felt a droll smile slide over her lips and re-sisted the urge to fidget. "Does that line usually work for you?"

"It's not a line, Martha Ann. It's a compliment. Try to enjoy it."

And for the first time in two weeks, he continued on his walk without inviting her to dinner. Had he given up? she wondered. Or lost interest?

Either way she'd been a fool.

AS IT HAPPENED, THE GUEST bedroom ended up being just the ticket, Finn thought on Wednesday evening. The lack of sleep the previous night combined with what had ended up being a very full day took its toll. And though he was sure he could have mustered the strength for a little bed sport, Finn knew he needed the rest all the same.

He also wanted to give Sunny some distance. If they became lovers this time, it would be because *she* wanted it, not because he'd forced her hand. Did he want her?

With every fiber of his being.

Tasting her yesterday, feeling her curvy little rump beneath his hands, her breast in his mouth, seeing her come for him…

Perfect torture.

He ached for her, wanted to plant himself inside of her with an urgency and desperation that bordered on insanity. It was completely out of the realm of his experience. Desire he was used to, but this frantic bone-deep need combined with that never-ending tug that only moved him closer to her was not familiar to him. Sunny Ledbetter had that special something, that indefinable special quality that simply set her apart from every other woman. He'd sensed it as a boy, realized it as a teen and was absolutely certain of it as a man.

But he would not charm his way back into her bed. He would wait for the invitation and if it didn't come, then it didn't. And really, could he blame her?

He was leaving again in two days, heading to Afghanistan by way of Fort Stewart. The last time he'd left her, he'd had a choice and he'd made the one he thought was best for his future.

This time he didn't have a choice.

He owed Uncle Sam eleven months overseas and another three after that of contracted service. Though incentives to re-up had already been bandied about, Finn had resisted. The nagging sense of discontent combined with the death of his parents had left him feeling as if he needed to plot a new course. Though he had the odd aunt and distant cousins, Finn was essentially alone now and, while he'd always considered himself an island unto himself, he wasn't so certain anymore.

He wanted…more.

Atticus lay on the front porch of the house, his head resting on his paws, as though surveying all of his domain. The sound of laughter and waves drifted to Finn on the salty breeze and he inhaled deeply, a sense of peace flooding him. Sunny was currently down in Number Six French-braiding the Johnson twins' hair for a family picture and the Wilsons, who were in Number Nine, were roasting hot dogs over a fire. Number Four had tied a kite to his deck and the giant butterfly soared overhead, irritating the seagulls that swarmed around it. Tug was sitting on his deck, a book in one hand, a glass of wine in the other. The sun was melting against the horizon in a grand display of yellow, orange and purple, painting the clouds with color.

It was beautiful here, Finn realized, and completely understood the Ledbetters' stipulation that the inn should stay as it was. Once again the idea of buying the place planted a seed of expectation in his mind and this time, he didn't try to uproot it, but rather left it there to germinate.

Pity that Sunny didn't want to stay here, Finn thought, wincing with regret. He could actually see them here, running the inn together. Helpmates, lovers, friends…even parents. Was it a cosmic joke that their timing was always off?

At any rate, he had other things to think about. Like keeping Heath away from her.

As soon as Clint had arrived yesterday, they'd made the trip to the police department and put the restraining order in place. If Heath so much as called Sunny, they'd pick him up. Finn wished he could get a handle on what was driving the guy. For reasons that escaped him, he got the unsettling impression that Sunny was keeping something from him. When

he'd asked her if she could think of any reason—
any reason at all—that Heath would continue to try
and force a reconciliation, she'd hesitated just long
enough to make him nervous.

Rather than press her, armed with Heath's last
name and the office computer, Finn had done a little
research himself. Within minutes he'd done a com-
prehensive background check that listed everything
from Heath's credit score—the man owed *everybody*
and was several payments behind on that fancy car
he was so proud of—to an outstanding parking ticket
he hadn't paid.

A real-estate developer, albeit a poor one, Heath
lived above his means and was on the verge of
bankruptcy. Via his Facebook page, Finn had noted
several wall posts that boasted about a "big deal coming through," but those had been dated almost three
months ago, and Finn assumed the so-called deal
had gone south because Heath hadn't mentioned it
again.

Finn frowned. That would have been about the
time Heath had met Sunny, he thought, and felt a
tingle across his shoulder blades that told him he'd
made the crucial connection.

Heath was a real-estate developer and Sunny's
family owned the Sandpiper, a prime piece of land
that could be worth millions. If Heath had gotten

wind that the Ledbetters were considering a sale, then, as Sunny's boyfriend, he would have been the logical choice to handle the transaction.

Bingo.

No doubt she knew this, Finn thought as he watched Sunny lope down the Johnsons' deck and start toward him. He'd offered to man the office while she'd donned the role of hairdresser.

Honestly, there weren't many roles a person didn't don when they ran a hospitality business, Finn thought. In addition to cleaning the rooms, answering the phones, booking new arrivals and taking care of the departures, there were countless other things that cropped up throughout the day.

Sunny had dispensed first aid, provided directions to the local grocery store, added chemicals to the pool, inflated a swim toy, supplied Number Two with a tube of toothpaste, given clothing advice to Number Eight—the red bathing suit was more slimming— provided the answer to a crossword puzzle to a guest who was stuck and helped capture a sand crab that had wanted to see what inside the cottage looked like.

She did it all with her trademark smile, without complaint. Though he knew she didn't want to take over the business for her parents, he thought it was a shame. She was a natural at it. The constant onslaught of requests would have worn most people down, but she merely handled each need in stride and moved on to the next.

Meanwhile, she routinely checked in with her store, put out the occasional fire there and last night—while he'd been moving closer and closer to bed—she'd reviewed new designs her team had couriered over earlier in the day.

She was truly remarkable, Finn realized. And very talented. He'd been curious about Funky Feet as well and had checked out her company's website.

For the flip-flop aficionado, her store was the equivalent of shoe heaven. He'd seen flip-flops decorated in feathers, ribbons, beads and shells. Every color, every shape and size, and an entire line devoted to bridal wear—seed pearls, satin, more feathers. Another higher-end line was called "Foot Jewelry" and featured rhinestones and semiprecious stones. Utterly inspired.

She slowed as she drew nearer and regarded him with an uncertain look. "What are you smiling about?" she asked suspiciously. "Should I be worried?"

Finn slung an arm around her shoulder, noting that she was the perfect height and fitted the niche at his side as though it had been specifically designed with her in mind. "Not at all," he said. "I just think you're pretty damned awesome, that's all."

She flushed and lowered her lashes. "Recreational drug use is a bad habit, Finn," she tsked. "You should know better."

He gave her neck a squeeze and laughed. "I tell you you're awesome and you accuse me of being high. Wonderful," he said, looking heavenward. "Hardly the thank-you I would have expected, but..." He sighed as though she'd wounded him and absently scratched his chest.

"Thank you, Finn," she murmured dutifully. "I'm glad you think I'm awesome." From the corner of his eye he saw her lips twitch. "My plan for world domination is working."

"Come on, smart-ass," he chuckled, herding her toward the beach. "Take a walk with me."

FINN LACED HIS FINGERS THROUGH hers, his big calloused palm brushing against her smaller one. The sensation was easy and pleasant and, despite what had happened between them yesterday morning, strangely intimate.

Though Sunny had been given many compliments over the years, she didn't think one had ever touched her quite the way Finn's I-think-you're-awesome one just had. The sentiment was simple enough, but it was the look on his face when he'd delivered it that had made it so special. The wondering smile, the genuine awe and affection in his gaze, as though he'd just unwrapped an unexpected present…and she was it.

Her heart gave a little jump and a pleasant warmth settled in her chest. Both rattled an alarm in the back of her head—she was letting him get too close again—but she determinedly ignored the warning.

"Thank you for helping me today," she said, enjoying the wind on her face. Funny how she didn't mind running the inn with Finn there, helping her pick up the slack. She'd actually enjoyed it more than she would have ever thought, and it was hardly the drudgery she remembered from her childhood. Odd… They'd reached the edge of the surf, where the sand sank a bit, but didn't shift and the waves lapped around their ankles.

"You're more than welcome." He shot her a sheepish look. "I, er, like to have something to do."

"Really?" she asked with mock astonishment. "Gosh, I wouldn't have known that. I would have never guessed it given how laid-back you are."

He nudged her shoulder playfully. "Knock if off," he teased. "There's nothing wrong with having an agenda."

She snorted. "There is if you're on vacation. There

is if you've gotten in the habit of staying so busy that you don't know how to be still anymore."

He laughed darkly. "Ah, there it is again. I can be still," he insisted. "I just don't want to be."

"Which begs the question, why?" Sunny drawled. "*Why* don't you want to be still? What happens in the quiet that makes you so unbearably uncomfortable? I have a theory, you know," she mused, letting the comment hang out there, the perfect bait.

Predictably, the curiosity got the better of him.

He heaved an exaggerated sigh. A muscle jumped in his jaw, belying the easy smile. "All right, Dr. Freud," he said. "I'll bite. What's this theory?"

Sunny simply shrugged. "You think too much and you don't want to be inside your own head. Your thoughts are either going in circles or reaching dead ends and it's easier to get up and do something than to sort out the chaos of your mind." She paused. "I'm not condemning you, Finn," she hastened to add, then grimaced. "If I'd seen the things that you've seen, I doubt I'd want to settle down with my thoughts, either." She kept walking, but felt him slow beside her. She purposely looked toward the ocean. "It just breaks my heart though," she continued. "The boy I knew could have spent an entire day in a beach chair, just soaking up the sun and breathing the air.

He wouldn't have jumped up within five minutes, as though a hot poker had hit him in the ass."

Finn stopped, bent down and picked up a shell. He washed it in the surf, then pocketed it. "I'm not a boy anymore, Sunny."

"I know that, Finn." She squeezed his hand. "But when you've got an agenda on your vacation that doesn't include *actually taking a vacation*…then I think you need to see if you can find him again." She took a deep breath. "Let me ask you something."

His lips quirked. "I don't seem to be able to stop you."

"What were your plans for coming here? What did you want to do?"

He smiled, chewed the inside of his cheek. "I'm pleading the Fifth."

"Finn," she admonished. "Come on. Tell me."

He turned to look at her. Orange light from the setting sun backlit him in gold, glinted off his bronze locks. His eyes, that glorious blue she routinely felt herself drowning in, were guarded. Tense.

"All right," he finally said. "I did have a few things I wanted to accomplish."

That was a nice way of saying he'd made a list, Sunny thought. She nodded encouragingly. "Go on."

"I'll leave here Friday, go back to Fort Stewart and

by the end of next week, I'll be in Afghanistan," he said. "This week was supposed to be about getting my head ready for that, for preparing me for what was coming at me for the next eleven months."

Sunny swallowed past the instant panic in her throat. *Eleven months?* She hadn't realized he'd be gone for so long. Her suddenly racing heart constricted in her chest and nausea roiled in her gut. That he'd be—

"This is the first time I'll ship out and won't be able to expect a letter from home, or a care package from my mother. My dad won't keep me updated on college football, how my Dawgs are doing," he said with a mangled laugh. "There will be no one for me to call and no one waiting for me when I get off the plane after it's all over." He shrugged, couldn't meet her gaze anymore. "I never realized how much I counted on that until it wasn't there anymore," he said. "It's all sort of left me feeling…off. Without a tether." Another weak laugh that tore at her heart. "So the next thing on my list was to figure out why. The career has always come first, you know? Next assignment, next promotion, next mission." He shook his head. "In light of what's happened, it all just seems so…insignificant. I feel like I've missed the point of an important lesson and I still don't know what it is."

Sunny couldn't speak past the lump in her throat and she blinked back tears, determined not to let him see them. He would mistake them for pity. He hadn't told her any of this to garner sympathy, but had shared it all in a glib, hollow tone that only seemed to make it worse.

He squeezed her hand. "I came back here because some of the happiest memories of my childhood—of my parents—are here," Finn told her.

He came to be closer to them, she realized.

"And I want you to know something else. Even if you hadn't been here, Sunny, I'd planned on tracking you down in Savannah."

She blinked, startled, and looked up at him.

"To apologize," he said at her blank look. "That's weighed on me much more heavily than you'll ever know."

In light of everything else he had going on, his broken promise made a dozen years ago hardly signified. Hell, no wonder he didn't want to be in his own head, Sunny thought. He'd just given her a tiny peek into it and she was ready to bolt into action, to do something to make her forget about it, as well.

Finn looked up at the sky, where the sun was just resting on the ocean and a smile she wouldn't have imagined him capable of at the moment spread across his lips. He sighed and pulled her more firmly against his side. "Would you look at that sunset," he said, marvel and wonder in his voice. "I bet you don't ever get tired of that, do you?"

She swallowed and shook her head. No, she didn't, it was true. The close of the day happened the same way every day. The sun made its usual descent, going to illuminate the other side of the world. But there was nothing common or even ordinary about the unique way the colors changed, the way the clouds moved through the fading light.

Sunny rested her head against him, slid an arm around his waist. She swallowed tightly. "Finn?"

"Yeah?"

"I'll write."

8

I'LL WRITE.

Hours later, Finn still felt those two words buoying him up and, though he'd merely responded with an inarticulate grunt, Sunny would probably never understand just how much the too casually uttered promise meant to him.

That someone would think about him while he was gone; that at some point during her day, Sunny would sit down and, with him in mind, jot a note and let him know what was going on in her life, was suddenly very important to him. It was a little thing, but it was those little things that people seemed to always take for granted.

He resolved to stop taking *anything* for granted. To appreciate everything. Every minute spent with a friend, every laugh, every beautiful minute of every blessed day. Life was too short not to, Finn thought, and he probably knew that better than a lot of people.

After that somewhat awkward yet strangely therapeutic conversation, he and Sunny had continued their leisurely stroll, then had made the return trek to her house, and he'd thrown those steaks he'd had on the grill. When Sunny wasn't looking, he'd tossed a couple of bites to Atticus and the dog had rewarded him by bathing his foot in spit.

Currently, Sunny was reviewing more work that had come over from Funky Feet and he'd taken a seat on the other end of the couch, *Harry Potter and the Chamber of Secrets* in hand. The book was fabulous—incredibly addictive. It had been a long time since he'd fallen into a good book; he'd forgotten just how much he loved to read.

"All right," he heard Sunny say with an irritated huff.

Finn looked up, not certain what he could have done, then realized that Atticus was doing his I-need-to-mark-my-territory march back and forth from Sunny to the back door.

Before Sunny could rearrange her paperwork, Finn set the book aside and hopped up. "I'll take him," he told her.

"You don't have to do that."

"I don't mind," Finn said.

Honestly, despite the fact she'd told him he could have the guest bedroom, he'd half expected her to try and send him back to his own cottage, based on the argument that she had the restraining order now.

She hadn't, and he didn't want to give her any reason to suggest it.

Finn was determined to stay with her, both for her protection and because… Well, because he wanted to. He wanted to be with Sunny. He felt right, for lack of better description, when he was with her. She plugged the hole, made him feel complete again. The desire was there, of course, ever-present and never-ending, but his need went beyond that.

Take now, for instance. She'd showered after dinner and donned a pink tank top and matching drawstring bottoms. Oink was screened across the front of the top, and the pants were covered in happy pigs rolling in mud. They were hysterical and, though there was nothing piglike about Sunny, the pajamas suited her.

At some point she'd changed her toenail polish from hot pink to bright green and the scent of coconut and pineapple clung to her dewy skin. Her nose was so squeaky clean it glowed and her hair lay in long damp curls around her face. There was nothing overtly sexy or seductive about the way she looked right now—Victoria's Secret would certainly pass—but to Finn, whose loins had been consigned to the fiery pit of the damned since the moment she came back downstairs, she looked *mouthwatering.*

In the first place, she wasn't wearing a bra. The pert globes of her breasts sat on her chest like plump, ripened pears just waiting to be picked. He wanted to lick them and suck them and rub his face between them. He wanted to watch them bounce on her chest as he plunged into her.

In the second place, he'd seen the single strand of elastic ride up the top of her hip above the pajama bottoms when she'd sat down—yes, he'd been trying to look at her ass—and was familiar enough with women's underwear to recognize a thong when he saw one. That meant her wonderful, lush ass was virtually naked and the patch of fabric that covered her front? Insignificant.

Hell, she could have been wearing a garbage bag and he'd have wanted her. Because he found *her* sexy. Just Sunny. *She* was what did it for him.

"Thanks, Finn," she said, smiling gratefully up at him. "His leash is by the door."

Struggling to pull his thoughts back into focus, Finn nodded and called the dog. Atticus hurried ahead of him, pressing his slobbery face against the screen. He clipped the lead into place and then followed along in the dog's wake. To Finn's disgust, Atticus didn't just need to mark his territory, he needed to make a deposit as well, a big steaming pile of it that he ultimately covered up with a few paw-fulls of sand.

"Your dog is having an identity crisis," Finn called upon their return. "He thinks he's a cat."

He heard Sunny chuckle, but the laugh didn't come from where he expected. It came from upstairs. He frowned. "Oh? How's that?"

Was she turning in already? Finn wondered, unreasonably disappointed. He'd been going to suggest a movie.

"He covers his—" Finn struggled to find the least offensive term.

"Oh," she said knowingly, laughing. "Yeah, he's always done that." A pause then. "Would you lock up? I'm in bed."

Damn. "Yeah, sure."

Though he wasn't exactly tired yet, Finn didn't see the point of staying up without her. It felt weird. He'd shower, then pass the rest of the evening with his book. He made quick work of securing the house, then made the journey upstairs. He'd brought a change of clothes and his toiletries over earlier in the afternoon and put them in the guest bedroom. Sunny's door was closed as he passed, which he found surprising. He was under the impression that, while he produced too much spit to actually sleep in the bed with her, Atticus slept in her room.

With a mental shrug, he walked into the guest bedroom and drew up short.

Sunny *was* in bed.

His.

And she was naked.

He felt a long, slow smile slide over his lips. "What happened to the voodoo priestess and the live chicken?"

"That was to get you into *my* bed," she clarified. "You didn't ask what it would take to get me into yours."

"Damn," he said with feigned regret. "I never ask the right questions." He grinned and quirked a brow. "Can you give me five minutes? I need to take the fastest shower in the history of the world."

It only took three and it still felt like an eternity. Miracle of miracles, Sunny was still waiting for him when he walked back into the room. He hadn't bothered with underwear, but had just secured the towel around his waist. Her eyes widened appreciatively when she saw him.

"When did you get the tattoo?" she asked.

Finn bent over and snagged a few condoms from

his toiletry bag and set them on the nightstand. "Right after Jump School."

"Why not a four-leaf clover?" she asked. "Why the three?"

"Because luck didn't have a damned thing to do with me getting through that," Finn said. "It was nerve, skill and determination." He shrugged, grinned. "And I'm Irish, so…"

She sat up and the sheet slipped down, baring her to the waist, revealing the prettiest pair of breasts he'd ever seen. She slid a finger over the clover positioned on the front of his hip, then leaned forward and traced the outline of the tattoo with the tip of her tongue.

He shuddered.

"Clover is edible," she breathed against his skin, kissing his hip. "Did you know that?"

"I—"

She gave the towel a gentle tug, sending it to the floor, then wrapped her hand around his shaft and licked slowly down the side of his penis. "Though I prefer this," she murmured in foggy tones, and took the whole of him into her mouth.

Sweet mother of—

Finn locked his legs and his jaw, then groaned loudly against the onslaught of sensation. That beautiful mouth wrapped around his dick, her facile tongue lapping at him… He fisted his hands at his sides because he knew it would be bad form to fist them into her hair and wondered how in the hell he was going to get through this without completely losing control.

Her small hand worked the base of his shaft while her mouth did unspeakable things to the top. She left off and laved his balls, then returned to the sensitive skin just beneath the head of his dick. She licked and sucked and periodically looked up at him, her eyes sleepy and sated, as though tasting him was as satisfying to her as it was to him.

It was that look that simply did it for him, knowing that she wanted him, knowing that she needed him as much as he needed her.

Feeling impending release building in the back of his loins, Finn gently moved her back onto the bed. "Let me, Sunny," he said, gently opening her thighs. He hooked her legs over his shoulders, spreading her before him, then with a hungry moan fastened his mouth between her legs. The taste of woman exploded on his tongue as he laved her clit and he sighed with satisfaction. Her back arched off the bed and she held on to the sheets to keep herself there. His tongue against her clit, he slipped a finger deep inside and began to stroke, and with the other hand, found a nipple and began to roll it rhythmically between his fingers.

He heard her gasp, felt her stomach deflate and smiled against her. "You taste so good," he murmured against her. Stoking, laving, tweaking. He increased the tempo and could hear her labored breathing, music to his ears, affirmation.

"Not without you again," she gasped, grasping his shoulders. "Please. I need—"

He needed, too. He grabbed a condom from the nightstand, pulled it from the foil and swiftly rolled it into place. A second later he was poised between her thighs, nudging her weeping folds.

Hair spread out in a golden halo of curls, cheeks pinkened with desire, lips swollen from tasting him...

Incredible.

With a groan dredged from his soul, he slid into her, and just like before, visions of another path—one that included her and curly-haired children and beachside bonfires and a perpetually farting dog—rolled out in front of him.

Shaken but not surprised, Finn threaded his fingers through hers, stretched her arms above her head, fully aligning their bodies and angled deep, getting as close to her as he possibly could. She clamped her feminine muscles around him and he felt a corresponding contraction in his chest. The same sensation occurred with every greedy squeeze of her body around his.

She was forcing her way into his heart, Finn realized with a start, weakening his resistance with each blissful seek-and-retreat into her body.

And though he'd been taught to fight, never to surrender, Finn grimly feared this was a battle he'd already lost.

IF THERE HAD EVER BEEN anything more wonderful than their joined bodies—the hot, hard slide of him deep within her—then Sunny didn't have the presence of mind to recall it. Sleek muscle, sculpted bone, that sinfully carnal mouth. He was poetry in motion, masculine beauty incarnate. She could feel him in every cell of her body, moving through her blood, winding around her senses.

Why had she ever thought she'd be able to resist him? Sunny wondered. Why had she even tried? He wasn't just her Achilles' heel, he was her Achilles'... *everything*. There wasn't a part of her that hadn't ever been vulnerable to him.

Finn O'Conner owned her...and always had.

Yes, he was leaving. Yes, he wasn't permanent, the expiration date still applied. But ultimately, in the end—when he could walk out of her life and potentially *never* return—none of that mattered. She'd realized that today, when he'd bared his soul on the beach, when she'd promised to write. Ultimately, the only thing that mattered was making the most of the time she had left with him, savoring every moment and, for the time being, simply forgetting all the rest.

Finn bent his head and kissed her, his tongue plunging in and out of her mouth, mimicking a more intimate act farther south.

And he was so damned good at making her forget…

Palm to palm, the desperation in his touch, her nipples abrading his chest as he pushed repeatedly into her…

It was too much, too wonderful, too exquisite for her to bear. She felt the first flash of orgasm kindle in her womb, igniting a frenzy of sensation in the heart of her sex. The pleasant burn in her veins turned into an inferno scorching through her, sucking all the oxygen from her lungs, making her buck frantically beneath him.

She squeezed his hands, wrapped her legs more firmly around his waist and tightened around him as he withdrew, trying to hold him in, to keep him inside her. He was the key, she thought dimly, and any second now he was going to unlock something magical inside of her.

Sunny bent forward and licked his throat, a sleek path from the hollow to the side where neck met shoulder. She suckled, then took a little nip and he groaned and pounded harder.

Aha.

She did it again, coupling the bite with a determined lift of her hips.

The sound that tore from his throat was almost inhuman. "Sunny," he said, her name a warning.

"Finn," she shot back a bit breathlessly, which ruined the effect.

"Do you have any idea how good you feel?" he asked her, punctuating the question with a hard thrust. "How much I've wanted you?"

Sunny smothered a hysterical laugh. Oh, she thought she had a pretty good idea, based on the sheer delight bolting through her. She flexed against him, lifted her hips and felt something shift deep inside of her.

The first tumbler…

She inhaled sharply and bucked beneath him, urging him on. Taking the cue, Finn released one of her hands and slid his arm around her waist, lifting her up to move their bodies impossibly closer. The shift did something amazing and, with every frenzied, methodical journey into her body, he hit the sweet spot nestled at the top of her sex. Another tumbler gave way, then another, and with a final, brutal push the last one fell back, unlocking the most amazing orgasm she'd ever experienced.

She completely lost the ability to breathe, her back arched away from the bed and bright colored lights danced in front of her eyes. The room fell away, shrank until the only thing left was Finn.

Her Finn.

She tightened around him over and over and with each new contraction, the release seemed to intensify instead of decrease, making the sensation go on and on. She felt Finn stiffen above her, then he pressed deep and held, and a long, keening growl of satisfaction roared from his throat. He trembled above her, then bent and pressed a kiss to her forehead. A heartbreakingly tender gesture amid what had been the most primal, elemental sex she'd ever had.

And in that instant, strangely, it became the most significant.

9

TUG WASN'T ALTOGETHER certain changing his tactic was going to work, but Martha Ann had been a whole lot more chatty this morning when he'd spoken to her, so clearly his new not-asking-her-to-dinner method was working.

Foolish female.

Why were these games necessary? Didn't she realize how much time they'd lost already? Didn't she see how much he cared for her? How much he wanted to be a part of her life, to give her everything he was capable of giving? He baited his hook and cast his line again, the symbolism not the least bit lost on him.

The bad news? She was leaving in a week.

The good news? He'd always been one helluva an angler.

"So Clint will be here at ten, right?" Finn asked on Thursday as he shook a pillow into a case. He and Sunny were currently in Number Seven, only a bed between them, and though he'd taken her so many times he'd lost count last night, amazingly, he could do it again right now. He was either very virile or very addicted.

Hell, he could be both, Finn decided. The two weren't mutually exclusive, after all.

Sunny looked up. She'd put on a yellow strapless sundress, which had some sort of distractingly stretchy fabric across her breasts, and she was wearing a pair of tricked-out flip-flops. This pair was covered in silk daisies. She looked fresh and wholesome and sexy, a mesmerizing mix.

"Yes," she admitted slowly. "Why?"

"I was hoping we could get out and kick around the island today. Maybe go have lunch, then come back and beach it for a while."

She hesitated.

"No problem," he assured her. He smoothed the spread. "It was just an idea."

"No, we can," she said after a moment. "I was just going through things in my head. Thinking about who was checking out, who was checking in. So long as we're back by three, Clint should be fine. I just don't want him to get overwhelmed."

He grinned. "Are you sure? I could always go get something, bring it back and we could have a little picnic."

Honestly, it didn't matter to him. He just wanted to be with her. He was all too aware of how short their time together was and he wanted to cram as much into it as possible. Already the idea of leaving her was making him anxious inside, making his guts knot with uncomfortable dread. He'd always hated the goodbye part when he was leaving his parents— his mother's worried tears, the proud concern of his father—but this was a different kind of trepidation. It was knowing they weren't going to be breathing the same air, a prelude to an ache he'd never felt before.

Leaving this time was going to hurt.

"I'll have my cell phone," she said, "and can be back here in a few minutes if something big comes up." She brightened and sighed wonderingly. "Wow. I think we're about to have our first date."

Finn chuckled and rubbed the back of his neck. "Done things a bit out of order, haven't we?"

Her gaze dropped to his mouth and lingered, then met his once more. "Oh, I don't know," she murmured, her voice smoky. "I think we've done things in the order of most importance."

If she kept looking at him like that they were going

to have to change the sheets again on this bed, Finn thought. They'd never make it out of this room, much less to a restaurant.

"Come on," she said. "We've still got to stock the towels by the pool."

He blinked drunkenly.

Sunny grinned. "I like it when you look at me like that," she said, rocking back on her heels. "It makes me feel powerful."

He held the door open for her. "Considering your plan for world domination, that should make you happy." She was certainly rapidly dominating his world, Finn thought. The warning bells that should have gone off as that idea slid through his head… didn't. Interesting.

Thirty minutes later, they were tooling around the island in her Jeep. Sunny wore a huge pair of sunglasses and the wind whipped through her hair, sending curls everywhere as they drove around. He'd offered to drive, but since this was her stomping ground and she knew the best ways to avoid the tourist traffic, she'd commandeered the wheel. After pointing out various landmarks—the Pavilion, the Fort and the lighthouse—she finally wheeled the car into a gravel parking lot.

"The island's too small to have any best-kept-secret sort of places," Sunny told him. "It's only two miles long and less than a mile wide," she said. "But if it did have a secret, then Nancy's would be it." She winked at him and jerked her head toward the door. "Come on."

Finn couldn't identify the exact flavor in the air when they entered the little diner, but it was mouthwatering. It was a seat-yourself kind of place, which he liked, and the menus were tucked between the salt and pepper shakers and the napkin holder. Again, another plus. It meant Nancy was more about the food and less about the service. So long as the service wasn't completely lacking, it generally meant he was about to enjoy a good meal.

Sunny didn't even have to consult a menu. "I always get the scallops," she said and gave a little shudder of delight. "They're divine."

With that sort of endorsement, he didn't need a menu, either. The waitress arrived with a basket of hush puppies, quickly took their order and was back with the drinks in record time.

Sunny took a sip of her sweet tea and studied him over the glass. "I'm having a hard time getting used to the hair," she said, surprising him.

He laughed and ran a hand over the top of his head. "It's the classic military high and tight."

"It's still got some wave," she said. "But I miss the curls."

"They'll cut it again as soon as I get back."

Her eyes widened. "What's left to cut?"

"You'd be surprised."

She sighed and shook her head. "Shame."

Finn paused while the waitress brought their plates. "Heath had longish hair," he remarked thoughtfully, spearing a scallop. "Is that what attracted you?"

Her lips twitched and her eyes twinkled as she picked up her own fork. She released a breath. "You are just not going to let that go, are you?"

He wished he'd never laid eyes on the guy, to be perfectly truthful. He didn't understand it. Couldn't wrap his head around Sunny actually going out with that pansy-assed, opportunistic *nut* and the idea that she might have—

His brain seized, refusing to go there.

He shoved the food in his mouth, mildly noting that it was good, and tried to focus on chewing so he wouldn't choke on the rage that had suddenly invaded his throat.

"We didn't, Finn," she said, taking pity on him. "Not that it's any of your business, but…no." She swallowed, then chased a bead of moisture down the side of her glass with her thumb. "The relationship never progressed to that level."

Profound relief poured through him and he went a little slack in his chair. *Thank God.* The idea of another guy... Which was ridiculous, he knew. There'd been other guys. He knew that. Would more than likely be other guys, as abhorrent as the idea was to him.

But he was about to leave for eleven months, almost a year. How could he ask Sunny to wait, knowing that? In a perfect world, he'd do his tour, finish out his contract, then return here and take over the inn. He'd inherited a bit of money from his parents and there'd been a settlement, of course. He could afford it and he wanted it. He'd never been more certain of anything. It had taken some time to work his mind around the idea, but as soon as he had, the discontent, the sense of unease had fled, leaving renewed purpose in its place.

Unfortunately, while he'd been on the wrong track, Sunny had blazed her own trail and he didn't see how the two were ever going to meet.

"You haven't heard any more from him, have you?" Finn asked, struggling to retain the thread of the conversation.

"No. The police must have gotten in touch with him."

It was possible, Finn knew, but something about it still didn't feel right. Like the calm before a storm, he had an eerie premonition Heath wasn't finished yet. He was a cornered man who thought Sunny was the key to his financial solvency. He was desperate and desperate people were dangerous.

"You know he's in debt up to his eyeballs, right? On the brink of bankruptcy?"

Sunny stared at him. "What?"

He leaned back and crossed his arms over his chest, taking a perverse sort of glee in knocking another dent into Heath's tarnished armor. "I don't know how he's hung on to the car. I'm surprised they haven't come and got it yet."

"How do you know this?" she asked faintly.

Finn shrugged. "I ran a background check on him."

She set her fork aside and gave her head a comical shake. "What? When?"

"Yesterday," he admitted. "When I used your computer." He told her about the curious updates on Heath's Facebook page and relayed his suspicions to her. "I think he had designs on more than just you, Sunny. He was working it from a business angle, too, and when you kicked his ass to the curb..."

She glared at him. "That's *why* I kicked his ass to the curb, as you so eloquently put it," she said, her voice throbbing. She flushed and looked away. "Sheesh. I can't believe you did that."

Finn frowned, confused on several different levels. "But if you knew, then why didn't you tell me?"

Her mystifyingly irritated gaze found his once more. "I know this is a very difficult concept for you, Finn, but it was none of your business." She said the last few words slowly and deliberately, as though she were speaking to a half-wit. "Furthermore, it was embarrassing." She stood, tossed her napkin on top of what remained on her plate and mumbled something about the restroom.

Finn sat in shock, not altogether certain what he had done wrong. She'd had an ex who was acting like a potential stalker. He'd investigated. One plus two equals three, right? Where was the misstep? What should have set her off about that? What was embarrassing? He didn't understand.

But he was about to.

Finn tossed enough money on the table to cover the check and added a nice tip, then made his way to the back and knocked on the restroom door.

"Sunny?"

"I'll be out in a minute, Finn."

"Are you in there alone?"

"What? Yes."

"Let me in."

He heard an exasperated sigh. "Finn."

"Open the damned door, Sunny." They didn't have time for her to be pissed off at him, Finn thought. He was going to fix this the best way he knew how.

He heard the lock click and he instantly pushed into the little room, thankful that there was only a single stall. He quickly flipped the lock back into place and in that time Sunny had resumed her spot in front of the mirror. She was staring at him in the reflection.

He walked forward and wrapped his arms around her, enjoying the way they looked in the mirror together. Her curly hair against his neck, his hands over her belly. "I'm sorry," he said, breathing her in.

She gave a helpless laugh. "Do you even know what you're apologizing for?"

He froze. Was this a trick? Did it matter? "Of course. I'm apologizing because you're angry with me."

She chuckled softly and shook her head. "Finn." She sighed again, his name a plea. "What am I going to do with you?"

"Is that a rhetorical question or are you open to suggestions?" he asked, nuzzling the side of her throat with his nose. She smelled wonderful. Like lemons and sugar and sun. She turned her head and found his lips and he took the opportunity to fill his hands with her breasts. No bra, he realized, and that knowledge landed directly in his loins. She reached around and cupped his neck, simultaneously pressing her rump against him.

He was going to take her, Finn thought. Right here in this little bathroom.

With very little effort at all, he dragged the sundress down, revealing her perfect breasts. *Tan lines, pouting pale pink nipples...* She arched against him once more, an unspoken request, but one he was more than ready to answer. Need hammered through his veins and he'd hardened to that sweet point between pleasure and pain.

Mindless with desire, desperate to plant himself between her welcoming thighs, Finn quickly freed himself and lifted her dress. Another thong, which was quickly dealt with. He bent her forward and slid inside, shuddering as hot juices coated him.

It was at that unfortunate point that he realized he didn't have a condom.

Finn swore hotly and met her sleepy, fevered gaze in the mirror. "I don't have any protection."

"I'm clean and covered. The pill. You?"

"Just had a physical." Besides, the last time he'd had unprotected sex had been with her on that beach twelve years ago.

"Then what the hell are you waiting for?" she asked, wiggling closer. "Come inside me."

Finn drew back and then slid home, watching her face the entire time. She winced with pleasure, her eyes fluttered closed and she bit her bottom lip, as though this felt as good to her as it did to him.

Skin to skin, no barriers. Just him. Just her.

Perfect.

He quaked and his knees went weak. She tightened around him, a silent energizer, and Finn suddenly lost all control. "Look at me," Finn told her.

She did.

He bent her forward a little, reached around and stroked her front as he pounded into her from behind. She was hot and tight and wet and he wanted to take her until one or both of them went blind.

In, out, harder and faster, then harder still.

Her breasts bounced on her chest, absorbing the force of his thrusts, and she made soft little mewling noises that did something strange and bizarre to his insides. Finn stroked her faster and she worked herself against his fingers. Her skin was dewy, her mouth slightly open and her curls shook around her face. She was wanton and sexy and that heavy-lidded gaze clung to his, never wavering. She was enjoying the pleasure he was giving her and she wanted him to know it, wasn't ashamed or embarrassed by it.

Vixen.

She'd be the death of him, Finn realized.

She gave a little gasp, a verbal indicator that she was close, and he felt the first contraction grab at his dick. He slid his free hand over her ass, then gently pressed his thumb against the rosebud of her bottom, while his other maintained its position on her clit. Meanwhile, he angled high, deep within her womanly channel and seated himself as far as he could go.

She came for him.

She went rigid, every muscle locked down tight, and her mouth opened in a soundless scream.

She did not close her eyes, but kept them fastened on his.

Had anything ever been more sexy? Finn wondered as he stared at her. Had he ever been more turned on? More connected to another person?

No.

Only her. God help him, it had always been her.

Her violent release abruptly triggered his own, and for the first time in a dozen years, he came inside a woman, spilling his seed deep within her. Though he knew it was impossible—she'd said she was covered, after all—he almost wished she wasn't. That there was a chance it would take root. That they'd make a baby, a little miracle with blond curls and green eyes and her smile.

And with that fleeting but oh-so-telling thought, he knew that he loved her.

10

"AFTERNOON, MARTHA ANN."

Stationed in her usual spot on the beach, Martha Ann looked up with a smile, one that was tinged with as much delight as regret. Her gaze fastened on Tug's blue one. He wore a pale yellow T-shirt and a pair of old denim shorts, and his curly gray hair was pulled back in a low ponytail. She'd never imagined that she'd ever be attracted to a man with more hair than her, but he was living proof that it was true. It gave him a very European flair. Her stupid heart skipped a beat. "Afternoon, Tug."

"Did you have a pleasant evening last night?" he asked. He reached down and washed off a perfect shell, then slipped it into his pocket.

She nodded her lie. She'd watched an episode of *Golden Girls,* then trimmed her cuticles and gone to bed. If her life got any more exciting she was going to have to take some medication to calm her down. "You?"

"Not really," he admitted.

"Oh?" She was more interested than she should be, Martha Ann thought. Furthermore, the more she talked to him the more he'd be encouraged and she had no desire to lead him on. "Anything wrong in particular?" she heard herself ask.

He picked up a broken shell and tossed it into the incoming surf. "Just lonely, I guess. I never used to mind not having someone to talk to. There was always something to do, some repair to be made, a book to read, a movie to watch, someone to share the occasional meal. Everything was fine."

She swallowed. "What changed?"

He smiled down at her, his eyes crinkling around the corners. "I think I did. Doesn't every man when he falls in love?"

Her chest tightened and a green haze of jealousy clouded her mind. "You're in love?" If that was the case, then why the hell had he been flirting with her every damned day since she'd arrived? she wondered furiously. Here she'd been trying to spare his feelings and they were engaged elsewhere.

She was a fool. A romantic old fool.

He nodded, looking away again. "With the same

woman for the past ten years. But she wasn't available so I could tell myself that there was no way things were ever going to work out. I had no choice but to make do, to go on."

Irrational irritation surged through her. She couldn't believe she was counseling him on how to get his girl. Maybe that's all he'd wanted to talk to her about, in which case she could have had a steak last night instead of a pimento cheese sandwich. "You make it sound like she's available now."

"She is."

"Then what's the problem?"

Tug chewed the inside of his cheek and his gaze caught hers again. A knowing twinkle sparkled there, as though he were not only privy to every illogical thought in her head, but to some private joke, as well. "I think she's playing hard to get."

And with that parting remark, he winked at her and strolled away.

Playing hard to get? Martha Ann gasped as understanding dawned and her gaze darted to Tug's retreating figure. He turned then, and shot her a smile over his shoulder.

That image would be indelibly written on her memory.

"Dinner's at six, Martha Ann. I'm partial to your lemon pound cake."

She felt the blood rush to her face, staining her cheeks and she released a breath she didn't realize she'd been holding. Of all the arrogant, egotistical— Her mental tirade came to a screeching halt as another thought struck. He was in love with her? She let the thought settle around her heart and the pleasure that bloomed there pushed a wondering smile over her lips.

He was in love with *her*.

Damn expectations and old age, Martha Ann thought. Steak was definitely on the menu tonight.

WALKING ON SOMEWHAT WOBBLY legs, Sunny exited the bathroom and made her way to the front of the restaurant.

"Man, everyone is staring at us," Finn whispered, sounding pleased. "I bet they know *exactly* what we've been doing." He ran his hand possessively over her ass, just in case there were a few people who didn't realize that they'd been holed up in the women's restroom for the past fifteen minutes.

Her cheeks blazed.

She batted his hand away. "Cut it out," Sunny whispered. "Idiot."

"Ah, you've hurt my feelings," Finn told her. "I'll take my apology in kind."

Unable to help herself, she snickered. He was

absolutely incorrigible and, fool that she was, she loved that about him. Sex in a public restroom, Sunny thought. Clearly she had regressed a decade or she'd lost her mind. Her gaze slid to Finn and she felt her heart give a little squeeze. Probably a combination of both.

He climbed into her car and casually dropped his shades over his eyes. Sunlight glinted off his bronze hair and a smile of pure masculine satisfaction curled his wickedly carnal lips. He was confidently relaxed, the picture of a perfect badass and ridiculously, this gave her a giddy thrill.

Because he was hers. For the moment, anyway.

"You look pretty damned pleased with yourself," Sunny said as she shifted into gear and swung out of the parking lot.

He turned to look at her, his lips twitching. "You weren't complaining just a few minutes ago."

"Who said I was complaining? I'm just making an observation."

"Oh, good," he said. "Then you won't mind if I do. You have a beautiful ass."

Sunny choked on a laugh.

"No, seriously, you do," he insisted. "It's full and heart-shaped and fits in my hands just so and—" he sighed happily "—it's sexy as hell. I love it."

Despite the fact that she'd just lifted her dress

in a public restroom and they'd had wild monkey sex in front of the mirror, his compliment made her blush. Somehow a simple thank-you didn't seem appropriate.

She cleared her throat, wondering when exactly she'd lost her mind. "You've got a decent ass, too," Sunny said, feeling as though a reciprocal compliment was in order.

"Decent?" he asked, sounding disappointed. "I practically write a sonnet about yours and all you're gonna give me is a 'decent?'" He shivered dramatically. "That's cold. I think we need to find another bathroom so you can warm me up."

She rolled her eyes. "You are so full of shit. You know damned well that you're a walking wet dream. You've got the market cornered on sex appeal. You don't need me telling you that I've had fantasies about sinking my teeth into your ass."

Impossibly, the satisfaction that clung to his grin intensified. "You've fantasized about my ass? Seriously? When?" he demanded.

"Most recently? This morning, when you came out of the shower."

"You should have told me," Finn said. "I would have been happy to oblige."

She snorted. "I'm sure you would have."

"I think we should make a pact," Finn said, as though he'd just had an inspired thought.

"I'm afraid to ask."

"I think we should make a pact to tell each other these things every time we think of them. Little pick-me-ups, you know."

She chuckled. "I think you're just looking for a reason to talk about sex."

"You wound," Finn said, with an exaggerated frown. "Your mouth makes me hot."

She blinked, startled.

"See how easy that was?" he asked her, settling more firmly back into his seat. "I'd like to paint your body with chocolate syrup and lick it off, especially the dimples in the small of your back." He sucked his breath through his teeth. "Put a strawberry between your—"

"Finn," she interrupted as a flash of heat blazed through her sex.

He smiled at her, the wretch. His gaze drifted to her legs, which she'd clamped together. "Yes?"

"Stop."

He merely grinned. "Makes you hot, doesn't it?"

More than she would have ever imagined. And he was sitting there, cool as a cucumber.

That would not do.

"I love the way you feel in my mouth," Sunny

said. "Smooth and hard, and at some point before you leave here tomorrow, I want to tie you to the bed and ride you until my eyes roll back in my head and I shiver from the inside out."

She peeked at him from the corner of her eye and, gratifyingly, he'd gone completely still. And judging from the impressive bulge in the front of his shorts, completely hard. She preened.

He was right. This *was* fun.

He put his hand on her thigh and started edging the dress up her leg. She swatted him away, but not before her breathing hitched.

"Are you insane? I'm driving here."

"Pull over."

"No. This is why your pact suggestion is a bad idea. We'll never get anything done."

His smile was truly wicked. "Oh, yes we will."

Her lips twitched. "Well, besides that."

He shrugged unrepentantly. "My argument stands."

"What am I going to do with you?" Sunny asked again, shaking her head.

His eyes widened significantly. "Are you deaf? I've been making suggestions and, for the record, I am wholly on board with that last one of yours."

His eyes went all smoky, and that voice… Mercy. It sure made her quiver.

"Later," Sunny told him as she pulled into the inn parking lot. "I need to check in with Clint and the store, make sure everything is still running smoothly."

"Then we can head to the water? I want to rub oil all over your body. You've got a bikini, right?"

"Forget the pact!" she admonished.

He frowned innocently. "That didn't have anything to do with the pact."

"Oh."

"Are you okay?" he asked, the picture of innocence. "You look a little flushed."

"I'm fine."

"Do you need me to get you something cool to drink?" he continued solicitously, as though he were genuinely concerned instead of simply needling her.

"If I need something to drink, I'll get it myself," she said, glowering at him.

His eyes twinkled. "Self-service isn't necessary when I am here."

"It might be, if you don't shut up," she threatened.

He guffawed. "Sorry," he said. "I got a little carried away."

"I know, and that's so out of character for you," she deadpanned. She climbed out of the car and headed toward the front office. Finn, naturally, followed her. She could so get used to this.

"Any problems?" she asked Clint.

The teenager shook his head. "Smooth sailing, Ms. Ledbetter."

In a nanosecond she went from feeling like a sex goddess to an old hag. Of course she'd be a *Ms.* to Clint. She was practically ancient compared to him. At the ripe old age of twenty-eight. It was so depressing.

"Number Nine needs new batteries for their remote control," Sunny told him. "Can you take care of that please?"

Clint nodded once. "Sure." He started toward the door, then stopped just short of leaving. "Oh, the guy from the grooming service said he'd bring Atticus back by four."

Sunny stilled and her heart rate kicked into high gear. "What?" She looked around and noticed for the first time that her dog wasn't there.

"The guy from the grooming service came and picked up Atticus for his bath," he repeated. "He said he'd have him back by four."

Finn stared at her and as he took in her expression, went on red alert. "He wasn't supposed to go, was he?"

"No," she breathed, her mouth dry. "My vet clinic grooms him. He's used to them there."

"Clint, the man who picked him up… What did he look like?"

Seeming to realize that he'd made a huge mistake with her beloved pet, Clint had turned a bit green around the gills. "Tall, blond, had a spray tan." His panicked gaze swung to Sunny. "I'm sorry, Ms. Ledbetter. I didn't know, I just assumed that…"

Finn went behind the desk and stroked a few keys on the computer, then motioned for Clint to come around. "Was this him?"

Clint nodded. "Yeah. That's him."

When Sunny's mind caught up with the fact that Heath had taken her dog, something wild and awful snapped inside of her. She picked her purse back up off the desk and headed for the door.

"Sunny, wait!"

"That miserable bastard has taken my dog," she growled. "I've got to get him back."

"Sunny, you've got to call the police first. He's violated the order."

What was wrong with him? she thought wildly. Didn't he understand? "I don't give a damn about the order! I want my dog back!"

"I know," he said, leveling an unreadable look at her. "And I am going to help you get him back. But you have to call the police and let them know what's happened." He glanced at Clint. "They're going to need a statement from you, so you're going to have to hang around."

Still looking as though he might puke, the boy nodded.

"Give me two minutes," Finn promised her. "And I swear to you we'll find your dog."

While Sunny paced and watched the clock, thinking of all the horrible things she was going to do to Heath when she got her hands on him, Finn called the police.

"They're on their way, Clint. You tell them everything." His gaze shot to hers. "Sunny, dial Heath's number and hand me your phone."

"I KNEW YOU'D CALL," Heath said by way of greeting, his voice smug.

"You did?" Finn asked, his voice low and lethal. "How?"

A pause, then, "Where's Sunny?"

"Here's what's going to happen, Heath," Finn told him. "You're going to tell me where you are and I'm going to come and get the dog—"

"Oh, no," Heath replied with an irritating chuckle. Evidently, he was a lot more brave over the phone, safely out of what he presumed was harm's way.

"You're not calling the shots here, Slick. I am and I say—"

"—or," Finn continued as if Heath hadn't spoken, "when I find you, instead of merely putting a bruise or two on your face, I'm going to totally rearrange it for you, you understand? I'm gonna mess you up so much your own mother won't be able to recognize you. Those are your choices. I'll leave it up to you."

"Stop that," he heard Heath say. "Dammit, dog, what are you doing? That's Italian leather!"

Finn chuckled and shot Sunny a smile. "He's using your upholstery as a chew toy, isn't he?"

Heath choked, made a gagging noise. "What the hell—"

"Atticus has a bit of a flatulence problem, too," Finn continued. "Hard to believe you didn't know about that." He paused. "What's it gonna be, Heath? The easy way or the hard way?"

"It's going to be *my* way," Heath said. "I want to talk to Sunny."

"You know who wants to talk to you? The police."

"For taking the dog for a ride?" he asked skeptically. "I don't think so."

Finn tsked. "You violated a protection order, dumb ass. They're going to pick you up. You're going to go to jail. Probably end up as some guy's bitch," Finn added, laughing.

The line went dead.

Guess the moron hadn't thought of that.

"Can we go now?" Sunny asked impatiently.

Finn nodded. "You direct. I'll drive."

Predictably, she mutinied. "No, I want—"

"He'll recognize your car, Sunny. For the love of all that's holy, can you just let me have the lead on this, please? I swear to you we'll get your dog back."

"Before that idiot does something like dump him on the side of the road?" she asked, her voice breaking. "Before he gets hit by a car or someone takes him?"

"Yes," he said, because she needed to hear it. Now he just hoped like hell nothing made a liar out of him.

She nodded, seeming satisfied, and then hurried out to his SUV. She rattled off directions and he shot out of the parking lot.

"I'm going to hurt him," Sunny said. "I've never wanted to physically cause someone pain in my life, but I do him."

"I'll hold him, sunshine, and you can throw as many punches as you want."

Her furious gaze found his. "I'm going to hold

you to that." She paused and her lips trembled with a smile. Unshed tears clung to her lashes. "So Atticus was gnawing on his upholstery, was he?"

Finn nodded, grinning, as well. "And perfuming the air in his customary fashion," he added drolly. Heath must have been watching the place, Finn thought. He must have been waiting for them to leave so that he could make his move. Anyone with half a brain knew that Sunny loved her dog, that she'd do anything to get him back.

A weak laugh echoed up her throat. "Attaboy, Atticus. Way to fight back."

"I'm surprised the dog went with him," Finn remarked.

"He only looks vicious," Sunny replied. "He's not. He'd trot off with Jack the Ripper if he came calling, too. He only gets defensive when we're in the house."

"So he knows to guard you, but not himself."

She rolled her head toward him. "That about sums it up, yes."

"Has he been around Heath much?"

"Enough that he would have gotten into the car with him without a struggle." She looked away, dashed a tear off her cheek. "This is all my fault."

"How so?" Finn asked.

"I should have—"

"What? Taught him to bite Heath?" He shook his head. "You couldn't have foreseen this, Sunny. This is not your fault. You need to put the blame where it belongs—squarely with Heath."

"What kind of person steals someone's pet?" she asked. "What kind of person is capable of something like that?"

A desperate one, Finn thought, but didn't say. Because desperate people did stupid things.

"A crazy one," Finn replied instead. "With a death wish," he added grimly.

"We're here," she said. "He's in Building D."

Anticipation quickened in Finn's blood. He drove down to the right building, shifted into Park and looked at Sunny. "Let's do this."

11

Hours later, after searching everywhere she could possibly think to look, they still hadn't found Heath or, more importantly, her dog. She rubbed her eyes and blinked back tears.

Sunny was quite literally ready to tear her hair out and was getting angrier by the minute. She'd initially thought that she'd only wanted to hurt Heath.

Now she was contemplating murder.

Clint, bless his heart, had cancelled his date and assured Sunny that he would stay at the inn until her return. He'd apologized repeatedly and was desperate to do whatever he could to help.

To be fair, though she'd been initially annoyed, this wasn't Clint's fault any more than it had been hers. He was a kid. Heath was an adult who could be very charming and authoritative when he wanted to be. He'd walked in, known Atticus by name, and when the dog hadn't objected or shown any bit of fear, Clint had let her pet leave with him. It was an honest mistake. She wished he'd called to confirm, but he hadn't, and there was nothing to be done about it now.

Finn, she knew, felt equally helpless. He'd manned the vehicle and had driven for miles without complaint. If she said go back by the apartment, Finn drove to the apartment. When she mentioned Heath's office, he'd immediately pointed the SUV in that direction. She'd checked all of Heath's local haunts and the police had put out an alert on his car. They hadn't seen him, either.

Considering that Heath was in real estate and had the keys to any number of empty homes on and off the island, the frightening truth was…he could be anywhere.

After a moment she said as much to Finn. "This is pointless," she said. "I feel like we're wasting our time."

"We're not," Finn insisted. "People are ultimately creatures of habit and when they're in trouble, they want to be in a place where they feel safe. Usually, that's home."

She hadn't thought about her apartment or missed it once all week, Sunny realized. How odd. She loved her apartment. It was in an old factory that had been converted, with lots of soaring ceilings, exposed brick and hardwood. It was beautiful. But when she thought of home…it was her parents' house that came to mind. Was that normal? she wondered. She'd been gone for ten years now, hadn't used it as an address in a decade. Shouldn't the apartment feel like her home?

"What happened to your parents' place?" Sunny asked suddenly. "Are you keeping it?"

Finn sighed. "No, I sold it. I thought about keeping it," he admitted. "But every time I went back there, I felt like my throat was closing in, you know? It was too hard, being in that house without them."

"I'm so sorry, Finn," she said, reaching over to squeeze his hand.

He tugged her close and slung an arm over her shoulder. "I felt really guilty about it in the beginning, but I think I did the right thing. I've got some things of theirs in storage, keepsakes and such. Dad's chifforobe, Mom's easel. Things like that." He turned to look at her, his concerned gaze tracing her face. "I saw a painting of my mother's in my room," he said. "It's of us."

Sunny laughed softly. "She painted lots of pictures of us," she told him. "There's one in almost every room."

He smiled. "I noticed that."

"She gave one to my mother every year. There are some of just me at the house. Didn't you see them?"

He shook his head. "No."

"You can have some of them if you want," Sunny offered. "The paintings, I mean."

"No," he said. "They were gifts."

"And they can be again. To you." She paused. "I'm sorry this is ruining your last evening here," she said. "I had other plans for you, you know."

Finn lifted her chin with his finger and met her gaze. "I'm with you, Sunny. Nothing is ever ruined when I'm with you."

She swallowed past the lump that welled suddenly in her throat. "What time do you have to leave tomorrow?"

"I thought checkout was at eleven," he teased.

"I think we can bend the rules a little in your case," she told him.

His eyes widened. "You're going to give me special treatment?"

"You've already been getting it, or haven't you noticed?"

He smiled down at her. "Oh, believe me. I've noticed." He paused, turned serious. "I have to be back on base by five tomorrow afternoon."

So he needed to leave by three-thirty, Sunny thought. It was too soon. She wanted more time. She almost told him so, too, but stopped short. What was the point? They couldn't have it. This time he *had* to leave and she was better thinking that he *had* to than thinking that he *wanted* to. If she told him that she didn't want him to go and he didn't say he wished that he could stay, she'd be hurt. Better not to put either one of them through that.

They'd had a wonderful few days together. Rocky at first, admittedly, but they'd come a long way. She'd gone into his bed willingly this time, so she couldn't feel tricked or cheated. He hadn't made any promises and she wasn't expecting any.

Was she in love with him? Most definitely.

Was she going to ache tomorrow when he drove away? Yes, to that, too.

Would she recover? Probably not.

But that was an issue for another night—one when she was alone—and she'd deal with it then.

In the meantime, they were together, not in the way that she'd hoped, of course, but he was here with her now and that was the important thing. She wouldn't let Heath ruin that. She wouldn't let him have that kind of power.

Something Finn said earlier resurfaced. "'People go home when they feel threatened,' you said."

He nodded. "Typically."

If she didn't think of her apartment as home, then maybe Heath didn't think of his condo as home, either. "Do you think he might have gone to his parents' house?" she asked, voicing her thoughts.

Finn gaze sharpened. "It's entirely possible. Do they live on the island?"

"Yes, I think so," she said slowly, her pulse quickening with a new shot of adrenaline.

"You've never been there?"

"No," she said. "But his mother's name is Grace, I believe."

Finn flipped open his cell and dialed directory assistance. In less than a minute he had a phone number and an address. "601 Marion Street," he said. "Do you know where that is?"

"On the other end of the island," she said.

Finn put the SUV in Drive once more and peeled out of the parking lot. Seconds later the phone was back at his ear and he'd called the officer who'd helped her file the restraining order. He gave him Heath's mother's address. "We're on our way there now." A pause, then, "I'll try. I'm not sure about Sunny, though."

After he'd disconnected, Sunny, curious, asked him, "What are you not sure about?"

"He told me to restrain myself. I told him that I would try, but I wasn't sure about you."

She lifted her chin with grim determination. "That's because you're supposed to *restrain* Heath so that I can beat the hell out of him. I hope you haven't forgotten your promise."

Finn grinned. "Of course, not. But do you really think that's something that I needed to pass along to Officer Hancock?"

She grimaced. "I guess not."

"If his car is there, they want us to wait for them."

"Finn!"

"We won't, if you don't want to. I'm just passing along the message."

"I need to get my dog back."

"I told you we would, didn't I? Have a little faith. I've got a good feeling about this."

And his good feeling turned out to be right. Heath had parked his Lexus in his mother's backyard, but it was there all the same. To her delight, Atticus had chewed an enormous hole in the armrest and puked it up onto the floorboard. She was going to give him an entire jar of peanut butter for that, Sunny thought. And the shoes off her feet.

Sunny headed back toward the front porch, but

Finn stopped her with a touch of his hand. "You can't just go up and knock on the door," he whispered.

"Why the hell not?" Atticus was here, dammit. She was going to get him if she had to break down the damned door.

"Because if he's hiding, then she's simply going to cover for him."

Sunny was getting sick of his rational answers. "But—"

"We need to flush him out," Finn said, looking speculatively at Heath's car. Something in his expression intrigued her.

"How?"

Finn grinned. "Come on," he said, towing her around to the backyard once more. "I've got an idea."

And it turned out to be a brilliant one, she had to admit. Finn set Heath's car alarm off. Seconds later, Heath—obviously terrified that the repo man had found him—came hurtling outside. Before he could make sense of what was happening, Finn grabbed him and pinned his arms behind his back.

"Hello, Heath." Sunny drew her arm back and slammed her fist into his jaw, on the same spot Finn had nailed yesterday. "Where the hell is my dog, you rotten bastard?" she asked ominously.

Unbelievably, Heath smiled at her as though she

hadn't just punched him in the face. "Sunny, I need to talk to you about the Sandpiper. I've got investors ready to make your parents a very lucrative offer and I—" Heath winced as Finn tightened his grip on his arms.

"Sunshine, I don't think you've gotten his attention the way you need to. Wanna try again?"

Finn was right. Rather than hit him in the face again, Sunny put her heel straight up into his groin. Heath gave a terrible choking grunt and would have crumpled to the ground if Finn hadn't been holding him up.

"Where's my damned dog, Heath?"

"What are you doing to my son?" an older woman demanded. "Unhand him, you ruffian! Before I call the police!"

At that moment, Officer Hancock arrived on the scene and Finn handed Heath off to him.

Sunny hurried forward. "I'm sorry, Mrs. Townsend, but is my dog inside?" Sunny peered around her, hoping that Atticus was on her heels, desperate to hear him bark or catch a whiff of his scent.

The woman blinked. "Dog? I don't have a dog."

Sunny's gaze shot to Finn and she felt terror bring moisture to her eyes. *Oh, God.* "Your son didn't bring my dog here?"

"No," Heath's mother said, seeming confused. "We don't allow pets in the house."

A sickening sense of dread balling in her belly, Sunny turned and glared at Heath. "What have you done with my dog?" she asked, her voice so tightly controlled she barely recognized it.

For the first time, Heath seemed to fully grasp the trouble he was in. He hung in his head. "The shelter," Heath wheezed brokenly. "I took…him to… the shelter."

Her horrified gaze flew to Finn's. "Come on!"

"REMIND ME NEVER TO GET on your bad side," Finn said after Sunny was reunited with her dog. She'd given Atticus the shoes off her feet as soon as they'd gotten back into his car and she'd piled peanut butter into something she called a Kong the minute they'd gotten home.

Home, Finn thought, startled. At some point this week, this place had become his home. He swallowed tightly. And he was leaving in less than twenty-four hours.

For eleven months, at least.

She looked up at him. "Why is that?"

"That kick below the belt," Finn said. Honestly, his own balls had shriveled up in pain after seeing that blow.

Sunny simply shrugged. "You said I needed to do something else to get his attention."

He chuckled. "True. Is your hand sore?"

"From the punch to the jaw?" she asked. "A bit."

"Let me get some ice for you." He got up from the porch swing and started toward the kitchen.

"I don't need it," she insisted. "It's fine. Thank you for today," she said. "You were great."

"No thanks necessary," he told her. "I was happy to help."

"I felt sorry for Heath's mother," Sunny said. "She didn't have a clue that he was in so much trouble, did she?"

He winced. "Apparently not."

"What will happen now?"

"I think that the trip to jail combined with the humiliation of his mother learning about his horrible behavior will be just the thing to get him off your back."

She shook her head. "I can't believe he'd pulled together investors for this property based on a few dates with me," Sunny said. "Was he out of his mind? This is my parents' place. Whatever they decide to do with it isn't up to me."

"He thought he had an in," Finn said.

She scowled. "He thought wrong."

"You're pressing charges on the dog-napping too, right?" Finn asked.

"You bet your sweet ass I am," she told him, nodding succinctly. She looked down at Atticus. "Nobody messes with my dog and gets away with it."

Atticus farted his approval.

Finn chuckled, unable to help himself. "Are you sure the peanut butter isn't what gives him gas?"

She released a long sigh. "Everything gives him gas. It's part of his charm."

That was one word for it, Finn supposed, but it wasn't the one he would have used.

She cleared her throat. "How long will it take you to pack up tomorrow?"

"Just a few minutes," Finn said, looking out at the ocean. Moonlight painted the silver sparkles on the water and the still of the night seemed to settle around him like a cozy blanket. This was where he belonged, Finn thought. Right here, on this piece of land, with her at his side. "It's thanks to my special training."

"Do you ever get scared?" Sunny asked. She rested her head against his shoulder.

"Will it ruin my status as a badass if I tell you yes?"

She squeezed his hand and chuckled softly.

"Nothing could ruin your status as a badass, Finn O'Conner."

He smiled into the darkness. "Then yes, I get scared. When I have time, that is. But I like it better when I don't have time. When I'm just in the zone, doing what I'm supposed to do."

"Is it everything you thought it would be? Being a Ranger, I mean?"

"Yes," he said, though he was ready to have a new life. It had been everything he'd thought it would be. He'd served his country with honor to the best of his ability. He'd protected democracy, the greater good. It gave him a keen sense of satisfaction, as though he'd done his part to further his country's longevity.

She was quiet for a moment. "So, no regrets then?"

Only one…and she needed to hear it. "I only regret that I didn't keep my promise to you, that I didn't write, that I didn't come back with my parents again."

She tried to pull away, but he held tight. "You don't have to say that," she said. "That's not what I meant."

"It doesn't matter what you meant. It's what you asked and I answered it honestly." He laughed to lighten the moment. "The truth is, you scared the hell out of me, Sunny, and I ran."

She leaned away and peered at him through the darkness. He could feel those expressive green eyes on him, probing for the truth. "I don't understand."

How to explain? "You made me want to stay, you see? I had a plan, I was supposed to be a soldier, I'd already gotten the scholarship. Everything was mapped out, ready to go. And then you and I…" He shrugged helplessly. "And suddenly I was having second thoughts about everything. Second thoughts, second-guessing. It was too late for that. I was eighteen, you were sixteen. It was too soon."

It was quiet save for the waves crashing against the shore. She absorbed his words. "Thank you for telling me that," she finally said, her voice strangely thick. "I needed to hear it."

"I needed you to know the truth. I know you thought that I simply lied to you to—"

"Get me naked," she supplied. "Yes, I did. I thought you'd used me."

"I didn't, Sunny. I meant everything I said. I was just too much of a coward to follow through."

"You were my first."

He nodded. "I know."

"I've never regretted that, Finn. Even when I thought that I'd simply been another notch on your belt, I couldn't regret it." He felt her swallow. "You've always been…very special to me."

"Then I'm honored." He paused. "And for the record, you've always been very special to me, too, sunshine. You make me feel—" he struggled to find the right word "—whole."

That was it, Finn thought. She completely him.

Sunny tugged him up from the swing and pressed a kiss beneath his chin. "Come on, soldier," she said, emotion clogging her voice. "It's time for me to give you a proper send-off."

MORE NERVOUS THAN SHE'D BEEN on her wedding night, Martha Ann, cake in hand, stepped out into the cooler evening air and made her way down to Tug's room. She spied two place settings and a bottle of wine and her mouth went bone dry.

"That confident of me, were you?"

In the process of flipping the steaks on the grill, Tug turned and grinned at her. Her stomach gave a flutter. "You're a smart woman, Martha Ann. I knew you'd come around."

He took the cake from her, then leaned forward and pressed a kiss to her cheek. His lips were soft and warm and she caught the scent of his aftershave, something salty and resinous like a windswept pine. He let out a long breath. "I've been waiting a long time to do that."

She blushed. "You gave me a lot to think about this afternoon," she said.

He set her cake on the table and poured her a glass of wine, then handed it to her. "The subtle approach wasn't working and I only had a week left to work with. I couldn't let you leave and miss my chance." He quirked a brow. "Is it too soon, Martha Ann? Are you still grieving?"

If Tug had been watching her for the past ten years then he knew that it wasn't too soon. She'd loved Sheldon because she believed you could choose to love when you had to. She'd promised to love Sheldon when she'd married him and she thought that she'd done that to the best of her ability. But she hadn't been *in love* with Sheldon in a very long time. Though she'd mourned his passing and even missed him to some degree, his death hadn't left her so bereaved that she didn't know how she was going to carry on.

In truth, she'd been managing on her own for so long—even when he was alive—that his death hadn't required that much of an adjustment. Sadly, just fewer meals, less laundry and less criticism. She'd grieved more because her kids had lost their father, because the grandchildren were in pain.

Martha Ann finally looked up and shook her head

sadly. "It's not too soon, Tug. But it's not going to work, regardless."

He stared at her, his gaze calm and soothing, as though he'd predicted this response, as well. "Why not? You're here, so I'm assuming that you like me well enough."

She chuckled. "I like you well enough," she admitted.

His twinkling blue gaze warmed with pleasure. "Then what's the problem? I'm an adult, you're an adult. We're not in the nursing home yet, you know."

All true, she knew.

"Is it your family? Do you think your kids wouldn't approve?"

A thought struck. "Do you have kids?"

"No," he said. "And that's a regret that I live with every day. But I don't want to live without you anymore and if I don't make you mine, it's just going to be one more thing added to that list."

"Tug," she admonished, looking away.

He slipped a finger under her chin and made her look at him. "I'm serious, woman. We're too old to play games—" he gentled his voice "—but we're not too old for love. Your kids wouldn't begrudge you a little bit of happiness, would they?"

"No. Of course not." She hesitated. "But it would be an adjustment."

He caressed her cheek reverently and she responded to the emotion in his touch. It had been so long since a man had looked at her that way, made her feel like her bones were melting. "Then let them adjust, Martha Ann. Give us a chance, would you? Let me love you."

Let me love you.

She swallowed. "And what of you? Don't you need to be loved?"

His gaze caught and held hers and he gave a little smile. "It'd be nice," he said, making her smile. "But all I truly need is you."

He slid a finger over her bottom lip, then bent his head and kissed her. Heat boiled up beneath her skin and warmth glowed instantly around her heart.

All right, Martha Ann thought. She'd let him love her and she fully expected to love him in return.

_12_

HER HEART IN HER THROAT, Sunny tugged Finn into the house and paused in the kitchen to get a bottle of chocolate syrup from the cabinet.

Finn saw it and chuckled wickedly. "You were listening earlier then," he said, pleased.

"Who says this is for you to lick off me?" she asked, shooting him a look over her shoulder as she led him upstairs.

His face went comically blank and she laughed as he said, "You mean…?"

"You might have the market cornered on sex appeal, but you don't have it covered on chocolate syrup and sexual fantasies."

"But I thought—"

She shoved him backward onto the bed, then straddled him. "That was your first mistake," she said, licking a path along his neck because she knew he liked it. "You don't need to think."

Sunny tugged her dress over her head and cast it aside, then leaned forward and kissed him, all the while slipping his shirt up over his chest. She loved the way he felt beneath her hands, warm and solid, sleek and muscular. His body was a veritable playground and she was ready to ride. She felt him harden beneath her and smiled against his mouth.

"Get naked."

"You're bossy. Interestingly, I like that."

"Good, because you're about to take a few orders. The first of which is to shut up."

He blinked. "What?"

"You talk too much." She put a breast a hairbreadth from his nose. "There are other things you could be doing with your mouth."

He opened it to say something else and she popped her nipple inside before he could.

He sighed and suckled, slipping his hands up over her back, mapping her spine. His hands were huge and made her feel small and cherished and protected. She loved the way they felt against her skin and told him so.

"I—"

She moved the other breast to his mouth before he could speak again, then reached down and started working his shorts and boxers off. For someone who was used to following orders, he was amazingly slack about doing so with her. "I thought I told you to get naked. You didn't." She tsked. "For that, you will have to be punished."

Finn didn't look the least bit worried. He flattened the crown of her breast deep into his mouth and a reciprocating tug started low in her womb. For a moment she forgot that she was supposed to be in charge, then remembered herself and snagged the chocolate from the nightstand. She put a dollop on his chest and bent forward and licked it slowly off, catching a male nipple in her mouth and giving it a tender bite.

He bucked beneath her, slipping his dick along her nether lips.

The sensation ripped the breath from her lungs and she lost her train of thought all over again. While she was trying to get it back, Finn dabbed some chocolate onto her as well, then began cleaning her up with his tongue.

Determined to keep the upper hand this time, Sunny parlayed this move with one of her own. She leaned forward, then slowly sank back, impaling herself on him one slow inch at a time.

The veins stood out on Finn's neck and he anchored his hands on her hips. "Sunny—"

She gritted her teeth. "Finn, what are you supposed to be doing with your mouth?"

He bent forward and suckled her again, and she began to writhe on top of him, slowly undulating her hips, then quickly finding a faster tempo. She couldn't help herself, she was simply obeying her body. He felt so good, so incredibly perfect. He was big and hard and she could feel him deep inside her, every ridge and vein, moving within her. He flexed his hips, meeting her thrust for thrust, then slipped his fingers into her curls and put a knuckle against her clit.

She rode him harder, tightened around him, creating a delicious draw and drag between their joined bodies. She felt the first quickening of impending orgasm in her sex and raced forward, determined to catch it. Her breathing came in little jagged puffs, her heart raced in her chest, and every cell in her body was focused on rushing headlong into release.

He suckled her again, applied the perfect amount of pressure against her and she came apart. Flew into a thousand little pieces. Sunny straightened on top of Finn, savoring the joy of release, and he continued to slide in and out of her, milking the orgasm for all it was worth. When he'd wrung every last bit of it from her, she collapsed on top of him and tried to catch her breath.

That's when he rolled her over and started the mind-numbing process all over again.

"FINN, I—"

"Now it's your turn to take orders," Finn told her. "Tell me what you want."

"I want you," she said, the simple statement burrowing into his heart.

"You've got me," he told her, and truer words had never been spoken. She absolutely owned him and always would. "Now tell me what you want me to do to you."

A wicked glint entered her gaze. "I want you to slide your hands all over my body. I want you to kiss every part that's white, every part that's pink and every part in between. Then I want you to come inside of me…and come inside of me," she murmured.

Holy hell, Finn thought, releasing a ragged breath. He smiled down at her. "You've got it, sunshine."

He withdrew and took his time, feasted on her breasts, then her belly, her sides and even the backs of her knees. He drizzled chocolate syrup on the small of her back and slowly lapped it up and had the pleasure of watching gooseflesh race down her spine.

"Cold?" he murmured.

"No, I'm not cold," she said, whimpering. "I'm

burning up in my own body. You're killing me, Finn."

He loved the way she said his name. It made him want to beat his chest and roar.

He looked up at her, up the long length of her body. "Do you want me to stop?"

Her green eyes flashed. "Don't you dare. Hurry," she pleaded. "I need you inside me."

How could he resist a request like that? He spread her legs, opening her to him, and slowly, deliberately slid inside.

Heaven, he thought, gritting his teeth against the onslaught of sensation. Had he ever been happier? Had anything ever felt more wonderful?

No.

Never.

And he instinctively knew it never would. Sunny was the only girl for him and always had been. He was more than a decade late and she'd moved on, made a new life, but it didn't change the fact that *she* was the one he wanted, the one he needed.

The one he couldn't have.

He couldn't be that selfish.

Finn pushed the unpleasant truth from his mind and pushed himself back into her, where he told himself he belonged. She wrapped her arms around him

and anchored her legs around his waist and held on
to him, as if she were clinging to the idea of them as
well, as if she never wanted to let him go.

Could he ask her to wait for him? Finn wondered.
Could he do that to her?

Eleven months deployed, another three in the ser-
vice. More than a year. It was too much to ask. He
couldn't. Wouldn't do that to her.

"Do you have any idea how wonderful you feel?"
she asked him, her voice hoarse with desire. For
him.

"I couldn't possibly feel any better to you than you
do to me," he said.

Her breathing was ragged, her face flushed. Her
curls were tangled around her face, a golden halo.
Beautiful. Achingly so. "You're wrong."

"How would you know?"

She tightened around him, slid her hands down
his back and settled them over his ass. He quaked.
"I…just…know."

"Can we have this argument later?" he asked. "I'm
kind of busy right now."

She chuckled. "Really? I hadn't noticed."

"In that case, I'd better work harder to get your
attention." He gritted his teeth and hammered more
forcefully into her, pistoning in and out, angling
deep, getting as far into her as he could without

having to be surgically removed. She was wet and tight and her greedy muscles clamped around him, holding him inside her, making him feel loved, needed, wanted.

Less and less alone.

Gratifyingly, her eyes closed and she held on to him, breathing hard, her nipples grazing his chest. He felt his release building quickly in the back of his loins, but wanted her to come again—*needed* her to come again—before he did.

He put both hands under her hips and shifted her until her breathing changed and he knew he'd found the right spot. He pushed harder and harder, in and out, in and out. Fire burned in his lungs and it was all he could do to keep the orgasm at bay. Finally, blessedly, she screamed, a low, keening cry and her feminine muscles fisted around him.

He came then. Hard.

His vision blackened around the edges, the room swam out of focus and everything in his body went still and seemed to explode at the same time.

He shuddered atop her, filling her up with his release. He stayed rooted inside her, didn't move, waiting for the powerful quake to subside.

When it did, he slowly withdrew, then rolled to her side and tucked her against his chest. She fitted perfectly there, as though that niche had been created with her in mind.

"Sunny?" he said, his voice rusty.

"Yeah?"

"I'm going to miss you." *I love you. I don't want to leave you. I want to stay. I want to marry you and have children and grow old together.*

"I'm going to miss you, too, Finn."

He sighed, the weight of everything he wished he could say sitting firmly on his chest. "You don't know how much I wish I didn't have to leave tomorrow." He wasn't making her a promise, Finn told himself, merely stating a fact. He could share that one, right? He could tell her that he'd rather be with her than anywhere else, right? He wasn't asking anything of her, just apprising her of a harmless fact.

He suddenly felt something warm and wet hit his chest and knew it was one of her tears. "Oh, I think I do."

"Don't cry," he told her, giving her a squeeze.

"Don't talk about leaving and I won't," she sniffed. She kissed his chest, then chuckled.

"What's funny?"

"You're sticky."

He hummed under his breath. "Maybe we should take a shower."

She leaned up and peeked at him from beneath

lowered lashes. "That sounds awfully…tame. I had a little something more daring in mind."

Intrigued, he quirked a brow. "You do? What exactly would that be?"

"Skinny-dipping."

In the ocean? Finn thought, a bit shocked. That was daring. And dangerous. He didn't like the idea of using his dick as shark bait. After a minute, while he was in the process of telling her as much, she dissolved into a fit of wheezing laughter that made him pause.

"Not in the ocean, you fool," she gasped. "In the pool."

He paused. "You mean the one in front of the guest rooms?" He felt his smile widen with appreciation. "That *is* daring. How long have you been doing that?"

"For years," she admitted. "If you'd ever ventured outside after midnight when you stayed here before, you would have caught me." She slid a finger down his chest. "I shriveled up many a night waiting on you, you know?"

It was his turn to laugh. "Your parents would have throttled you, you realize that, don't you?"

She grinned at him. "I guess it's a good thing I never got caught then, isn't it?" She sat up and kissed

him. "Come on, Finn. Let's go play Marco Polo…
in the nude."

Well, when she put it like that how could he
refuse?

13

WELL, HERE IT WAS, Sunny thought miserably. The worst day of her life.

Naturally, it was a beautiful one. Fluffy white clouds drifted often enough in front of the sun to keep from making the umbrella a necessity and the surf was high, rolling in on waves that were made for ocean fun. The water was a lovely blue-green and had a clean scent to it that promised rain at some point later in the day. Sunny buried her toes in the sand and let her head fall back against her chair.

Though Fridays were typically busy days for the inn, today had turned out to be relatively calm. Finn had quickly helped her get through the morning chores and they'd brought their chairs down to the water. She'd donned her skimpiest bikini for him and was thankful that her mother and father weren't there.

They'd be appalled.

"I'm proud of you," Sunny remarked, after they'd been sitting there for an hour. She sipped her lemonade and savored the tanginess against her tongue.

He rolled his head toward her and smiled. "Let me guess? It's my stamina, right?"

She laughed. "No."

"My virility? My especially large penis?"

"Would you shut up," she hissed, looking around to make sure no one overheard him. A couple of kids were working on a sand castle nearby and Tug and Martha Ann were only a few feet down the beach, seeming as content as she and Finn were. "There are people around."

He grinned. "Sorry. I'll behave."

She snorted, though affection pushed her lips into a smile. "That's doubtful, but one can hope."

"Why are you proud of me?" Finn asked, seemingly intrigued. "I'm curious now."

She released a slow sigh. "Because we've been sitting here for more than an hour and you haven't jumped up to play in the sand or swim or help someone fly a kite or…anything. You've been content."

"That's because I'm with you," he said, as though it should be obvious. "It's easy to be still when you're around." He slid her a smile that made the top of her thighs catch fire and her belly quake. "Well, except for when I'm licking chocolate sauce off your—"

"Shut up," she said through clenched teeth. "Honestly, Finn. You're incorrigible."

He nodded once, seeming humbled. "Thank you."

She rolled her eyes, exasperated. "It wasn't a compliment."

He blinked. "But you were smiling."

"That's to keep from screaming."

He waggled his brows. "I like it when you scream. Especially my name. It makes me feel like I can conquer the world."

What was she going to do without him? Sunny thought with furious despair. She loved his outrageous sense of humor, the shocking things he said. They made her tingle and glow inside and she knew that light was going to go out again as soon as he left. He was going to have to say it soon, too.

She knew it. Could feel it coming.

He'd already packed everything other than what was right here with him on the sand, but their time together was still closing in on them, circling and circling, getting smaller by the minute.

Tears pricked the back of her lids, but she blinked

them away, determined not to cry. At least until after he left, anyway.

"So when are your parents supposed to be back?" Finn asked.

"Tomorrow," she said, swallowing.

He didn't look at her, but studied the ocean. "And you'll go back to Savannah?" The question was uttered casually, as though her answer was insignificant, but the air suddenly changed around them.

She nodded. How bizarre, Sunny thought. To think of resuming her old life when, for reasons which escaped her, it felt like it belonged to someone else, someone she wasn't anymore. How could that be? Sunny wondered. How could she have changed so much over the past five days? How could everything she'd worked for, everything she'd wanted, shift so dramatically?

But the person she wanted to be—the person she was certain she was *meant* to be—was sitting right here with Finn. If she could have him, she'd want to stay here, Sunny realized, the idea blooming into the perfect dream. She'd want to stay here and build a life with him. Have a family with him. A vision of a bronze-haired little boy with Finn's impish smile rose in her mind's eye and she instantly—irrationally—loved that child, missed him even though he'd never existed.

How was that possible?

Something started to tear inside of her and she wrapped her arms around her chest to keep the pieces together. Swallowed back the sob that rose in her throat.

She couldn't make it hard on him, dammit. It wasn't fair. He was about to go off to war, to fight, possibly never to return—nausea clawed up her throat at the thought—and it wasn't right to make him worry about hurting her, make him feel even more powerless than he already did. It was enough to know that he didn't want to leave her, to know that he would stay this time if he could.

Finn was quiet for a long time, but reached over and threaded his fingers through hers. Seagulls squawked overhead and the sound of the surf pounded against the shore. Kids laughed and parents cautioned and it was all familiar, yet somehow very different.

Finn squeezed her hand and she knew the time had come. "I've got to get on the road," he said, his voice strained and reluctant.

She looked over at him and nodded through misty eyes.

He shook his head when he saw her tears. "Don't do this to me, Sunny. You know I don't have a choice."

She nodded, her throat thick. "I know. I'm all

right." She paused. "It's just been—" she struggled to find the right word, but none were good enough "—wonderful seeing you again. I've missed you," she admitted and gave a little shrug. Her gaze searched his. "You're my Finn."

"And you're my sunshine." He slid a finger over her cheek. "You always have been."

She stood, because she knew she had to. Because she refused to be pathetic in front of him. She'd known from the minute she'd seen his name on the reservation screen that he was checking in and he'd be checking out.

Nothing had changed and yet everything was different.

But that was the way it worked. People came here to vacation then returned to their normal lives. She'd be returning to her normal life as well, as dismal as it all seemed now. She'd go back to Savannah to her business, to her apartment that she loved but still couldn't call home. She'd find her rhythm again. She would. She had to, because she didn't have a choice. She glanced back up at the house, at the inn and her heart gave a squeeze.

Or maybe not, Sunny thought. Maybe she'd stay after all.

Finn gathered up his things and stowed them in the back of his SUV. Though he hated the sand,

Atticus ambled off the porch and came to see him off, as well.

Finn smiled when he saw her dog. "Take care of her for me," he said, and Atticus sneezed and expelled gas simultaneously.

Sunny laughed, which helped keep her from crying. It felt as if her very soul was shattering, as if at any moment it would crumble away inside her. "Listen, Finn. I told you I would write—and I will—but I'm going to need an address." She paused because her throat had tightened painfully. "You'll send me the address right?"

Something shifted in his gaze—regret, maybe? "I will," he said and his gaze tangled with hers. "And that's a promise that I swear to you I will keep. No more broken promises between us. Ever."

She nodded. "Thank you. That means a lot."

He opened his mouth, shut it again and seeing him struggle when he was ordinarily so self-assured made her ache for him. "I really wish that things were different, Sunny," he said, a nuance in his voice she couldn't readily decipher. His gaze tangled with hers. "I wish that I wasn't leaving. And I really wish that our timing wasn't always off."

The lump in her throat swelled. "Me, too."

"I'm going to be gone eleven months," he said,

and there was an undercurrent in his voice that she didn't understand, something that she was missing.

"I know," she told him, nodding miserably. "I'll write, I promise."

He hesitated. "Thank you." He stepped forward and framed her face with his hands, then bent his head and pressed his lips against hers. The kiss was desperate and reverent and held a wealth of unresolved emotion. He tasted like lemonade and maple syrup, home and family, her past, her future, her everything. He molded her to him and groaned and she felt the telltale bulge against her belly.

He couldn't do this to her. They didn't have time.

He tore his mouth away from hers and rested his forehead against hers. "Oh, Sunny," he breathed. "You don't know how much I wish we wanted the same things." He pressed another kiss against her lips, then hastily climbed into his car. "Write, please," he said, his voice slightly thick.

She nodded, wrapped her arms back around her middle, then watched him drive away. Out of her life. Again.

TELLING HIMSELF THAT HE'D DONE the right thing— the noble thing—Finn patted himself on the back for not being selfish and asking her to wait for him, to give up her own life to accommodate his. He knew, at some point, he wouldn't feel quite so gutted as he did now. At some point, he'd be okay again. He wouldn't feel as if his heart had been filleted, his very soul separated from his body.

He sincerely hoped that sensation came sooner rather than later, because frankly, he wasn't sure how long he was going to be able to stand this.

And he hadn't even made it off the island yet.

He wanted to be selfish. He wanted Sunny. He wanted to ask her to wait for him. Ask her to let him buy the inn from her parents so the two of them could run it together and make babies and eat chocolate off one another's bodies from now until death do they part.

That's what he wanted. What he knew was right for him.

But was it right for her? When she'd specifically told him that the inn had stolen her childhood, that it had been her parents' dream and not hers? Hadn't he told her that she was allowed to have different dreams?

Yes.

But he still felt cheated. Because if he'd taken the path with her all those years ago, things would have been different. They would be together. They'd probably already have a family. They would have been happy.

And he wouldn't feel this damned, miserable gaping hole in his chest.

Again.

Yes, he'd gone back to the Sandpiper because it held wonderful memories for him, because he'd wanted to honor his parents in some strange way, but he knew now that it had been more than that.

It had been Sunny.

It had *always* been Sunny.

He'd wanted to get back to her, to the man he was when he was with her. He'd made a huge mistake all those years ago, one he could have righted when she'd been old enough…but he hadn't. The more time had passed, the easier it had been to simply let it go. Had he come back, even two years later, he knew that they would have worked things out. He would have proposed and she would have accepted and their lives would be vastly different now.

But he couldn't rewrite history and he couldn't go back this time, even if he wanted to. Because Sunny had taken the path he'd forced her into and she was happy. Who was he to take that away from her? How arrogant was he to think that he could make her happier than she was now?

His cell phone rang, startling him. He checked the display, but didn't recognize the number. "Hello."

"Pull over."

Sunny? He frowned. "What?"

"Pull over," she repeated impatiently. "I'm behind you."

Finn's gaze darted to his rearview mirror and sure enough, there she was. His heart skipped a beat. Blond hair whipping in the wind, big-ass sunglasses on her face, Atticus in the front seat. What the hell was she doing? Why had she followed him? He inwardly groaned and wondered where he was going to find the strength to tell her goodbye again.

She was making it damned hard for him to be noble, Finn thought.

He quickly pulled his car over to the side of the road, then got out and hurried to the back of his SUV. Sunny had already whipped her Jeep over and was coming toward him.

"What did you mean?" she asked, pushing the hair out of her face.

"I'm sorry?"

She slid her sunglasses up, sliding them atop her head. "What did you mean when you said you wished we wanted the same things? What things? You never told me anything that you wanted. How do you know we don't want the same things? Are you psychic?"

Oh, hell. He'd said too much. He groaned and resisted the urge to move closer to her. To breathe her in. "Sunny, I'm trying really hard not to be selfish."

"Do you know why it's hard?" she asked, glaring at him.

"Because it's the right thing to do?"

"No, because it's out of character for you. What were you talking about?" she repeated, her gaze tangling with his. "And be specific."

All right, then, Finn thought, straightening. She'd asked for it. "I want you," he said simply, his gaze tracing the woefully familiar lines of her face, lingering on the freckle on her eyelid, the shape of her mouth. "I want you to wait for me. I don't want you to so much as look at another guy, much less consider going out with him. I want exclusivity for the rest of your life."

She gasped. "But—"

He shushed her, laying a finger against her lips and her eyes widened. "I'm not finished." His gaze searched hers. "I want to buy the inn from your parents and let them retire. I'll run it myself if you want to keep doing Funky Feet, though admittedly, I'd like it better if we ran it together. Or we can do both. Run the inn together and you keep Funky Feet." He shrugged as if it didn't signify. "Doesn't matter to me, so long as we're together."

"But I—"

He put his finger back over her lips. "Stop interrupting. It's rude," he admonished her, then continued. "I want to live in your parents' house and make a family. I want two kids—a boy and a girl—and another dog, a black Lab we can name Scout, and I want to buy stock in chocolate syrup and lick it off you anytime I want. I want to marry you the instant I get home." He was on a roll now, Finn thought. In for a penny, in for a pound. She'd asked, hadn't she? "Ideally you'll be waiting for me in a wedding dress. That would make things simpler." He nodded once and instantly imagined it. "I—"

She put a finger against his mouth, stopping him. "Let me ask you something, genius. Why did you assume that I wouldn't want any of that?"

He blinked. "Because that's what you said. You said—"

"When did I ever tell you that I didn't want to marry you? That I didn't want to have your children and grow old with you? When did I ever tell you that I didn't want to wait?" she all but howled, stomping her foot. "I've been waiting *twelve years!* Where in the hell did you get the idea that I wouldn't wait another *one?* Because I sure as hell never said that."

He was hopelessly confused. "But you said you

didn't want to run the inn, that you were happy with your life."

"I was," she said, her hands framing his face. Her thumbs slid over his cheeks. "I was as happy as I could be considering that I didn't have you."

He nearly melted on the spot he went so weak with relief. "So you'll wait?"

She kissed him. "I will, you fool."

"And you'll marry me?"

"The minute you get back. I'm hopelessly, irrevocably in love with you."

Finn whooped, then lifted her off the ground and spun her around. His chest felt so full he thought it was going to explode. The hole was gone again, plugged up by her. She completed him. Made him whole. "You are?"

She laughed and tears spilled past her lashes. "I am. I told you that you're my Finn. You always have been."

"And when I told you I was going to be gone for eleven months, you were supposed to tell me you'd wait for me."

"I was?"

He smiled sheepishly at her. "I'd hoped."

"How was I supposed to know that's what you wanted me to say?" she asked, her voice climbing. "You haven't given me any hint that you were thinking any of this."

"That's because I didn't think it was fair to ask you to keep sacrificing for me."

"And you thought it was fair to love me and want to spend the rest of your life with me and not tell me that? Dammit, I'm not a mind reader. After we're married, you're going to have to forget about being subtle and just lay it all on the line."

"In future I will not hesitate to tell you everything I am thinking." He smiled. "Even when it's inappropriate."

She chuckled, held him tighter. "I'm counting on it."

"And the inn?" he asked, searching her face. "We don't have to do that if you don't want to, Sunny. I just want to be where you are. We can live in Savannah. Hell, we can live at the North Pole if that's what you want."

"I fell in love with the Sandpiper again while you were here," she admitted, knowing it was the truth. And it was her heritage, one she was proud of. "I'd already decided to move back and let Mom and Dad retire. It's a great place to raise a family."

Traffic whipped by them on the highway and the occasional driver honked a horn. "I want to start one as soon as I get back," he said. "Be ready."

She wrapped her arms around his neck and smiled. "I'll have the chocolate syrup in my purse."

"What?" he teased. "No voodoo priestess and live chicken?"

She chuckled softly and the sound burrowed into his heart. "I love you, Sunny," he murmured. "You know that, right?"

"I do now."

"And you'll write?"

"Every day. I'll email, I'll call, I'll send smoke signals," she teased. "I'm here for you, Finn." She squeezed him. "Know that."

He tipped her lips up for one last farewell kiss, savored the flavor of her on his tongue. "I do," he said, realizing at that moment how important that knowledge was to him.

She was his. *Finally.*

And she'd be waiting.

Epilogue

Two months later...

> Looks like we're starting early...
> Love, Sunny

CONFUSED BY HER NOTE, Finn held up the small, grainy black-and-white picture that had been included in his care package and wondered what his fiancée had sent him. It looked like a picture of a big bubble with a bean inside. When she'd told him she'd included a surprise in his care package, he'd been waiting anxiously for it to arrive. Unfortunately, if he didn't know what the hell he was looking at, then he could hardly understand the significance, could he? He peered closer, trying to make out exactly what it was he was supposed to be seeing.

Justin Andrews slapped him on the back. "Congratulations, man," he said, smiling. "I didn't know your old lady was expecting."

Finn blinked, feeling suddenly faint, and looked at the little photo again, then read the small print at the bottom that he'd missed before. *Sunny Ledbetter. Gestation 9 wks.*

Looks like we're starting early, she'd said.

A baby. She was having his baby.

He jumped up and whooped loudly, then started shouting at everyone in the barracks. "I'm going to be a father! We're having a baby! A baby! Oh, man!" So much for her being covered, Finn thought. Evidently her birth control had been no match for his virility. He couldn't be happier.

Finn blinked back tears of joy and felt his chest constrict with the strangest, most powerful emotion.

A baby. *Their* baby.

His mom and dad would have been so proud.

Seven months later...

"I'M GOING TO THROTTLE YOU with my bare hands when you get home, Finn O'Conner," Sunny panted into the phone, her voice strangled with pain and irritation.

"Baby, you know you don't mean that," Finn told her, listening to every sound coming from the delivery room. "You love me, remember?"

She howled again, then made a grunting noise. "I'd love you more if you were here so I could knock the hell out of you!" Her voice broke into a little sob. "Why didn't I want an epidural? Why, oh, why did I think I could do this?"

"Because you wanted to be a badass, too, remember? You said you were tough."

"I'm not," she whimpered, breaking his heart with her pain. "I'm a wuss."

He smothered a laugh because he knew she wouldn't appreciate it. Only his Sunny. "You're not a wuss, honey. You're amazing. I love you."

"Shut up," she panted, rallying. "You're not supposed to be nice when I'm mad at you."

"Whatever makes you feel better."

She groaned again and he heard her breathing increase. "Oh, no, here comes another one."

"Push, Sunny," he heard someone say.

"Finn!" she screamed. "I'm going to get you! I'm going to gut you like a fish—"

"The baby's crowning," another voice cried. "One more push, Sunny. You're almost there."

"You can do it, baby," Finn told her, his heart

about to pound right out of his chest. A baby, their baby. He was about to be a father.

Another long growl of pain from Sunny, then an awed silence, then a beautiful healthy cry.

"It's a boy," his soon to be mother-in-law cried.

"I've got a son!" Finn screamed to the room at large and huge cheer erupted around him. "Sunny? Sunny?"

"He's beautiful," she sobbed, her voice tired and reverent. "Oh, Finn, he's so perfect. Our boy. Our baby. I don't h-hate you anymore."

He laughed, spent, wishing with every fiber of his being that he was there with them. *His family*. "I'm glad," he choked out. "I love you."

"You'll meet Cam soon."

"Cam?"

"Cameron Finn O'Conner," she said. "After your dad."

He nodded, unable to speak.

Two months later...

FINN WAS ON THE EDGE of his seat as the plane descended and out of it by the time it taxied to a stop. Though he knew everyone on board was anxious to get off and see their families, he was selfishly pushing his way to the front of the line, determined to be the first one off the plane. He bolted down the steps, his gaze scanning the crowd, and he stilled when he saw them.

She was in a wedding dress, just like he'd asked, but she'd brought the ceremony to him. Sunny was standing under an arbor, her parents next to her, Cam—his son—in her arms. Ferns and flowers and the preacher, it was all there, but everything else sort of drifted out of focus as he ran to her—to them.

His Sunny, his Cam.

"Welcome home, Daddy," she said.

Finn couldn't speak. The words lodged in his throat as he gazed at his son. He was perfect. He had bronze hair and Sunny's mouth and he was, quite simply, the most amazing little boy that ever lived in the entire history of the world. They'd made this little person, this perfect little being. Finn missed his parents even more. They would have been so happy.

"You want to hold him?"

He nodded, his throat tight.

She stroked his cheek, her eyes brimming with unshed tears. "You can't speak?"

He shook his head.

Tears streamed down her face and she smiled at

him. "You're going to have to choke out an 'I do' in a minute, okay?"

He did. And he didn't choke it out. His voice was clear and certain when he said the words. The words that finally told him he was home.

* * * * *

COMING NEXT MONTH

Available January 25, 2011

#591 NOT ANOTHER BLIND DATE...
Janelle Denison, Leslie Kelly, Jo Leigh

#592 BREAKING THE RULES
Uniformly Hot!
Tawny Weber

#593 TAKE MY BREATH AWAY...
The Wrong Bed
Cara Summers

#594 THE WILD CARD
Men Out of Uniform
Rhonda Nelson

#595 TURN UP THE HEAT
Checking E-Males
Isabel Sharpe

#596 HEAT OF THE MOMENT
It Takes a Hero
Karen Foley

REQUEST YOUR FREE BOOKS!

2 FREE NOVELS
PLUS 2
FREE GIFTS!

HARLEQUIN®

Blaze

Red-hot reads!

---

*Harlequin Romance author Donna Alward is loved
for her gorgeous rancher heroes.*

*Meet Wyatt as he's confronted by both a precious
little pink bundle left on his doorstep and his neighbor Elli
who's going to show him the ropes....*

Introducing
PROUD RANCHER, PRECIOUS BUNDLE

THE SQUAWKING QUIETED as Elli picked the baby up, and
Wyatt turned around, trying hard to ignore the feelings of
inadequacy as Darcy immediately stopped fussing.

"Maybe she's uncomfortable. What do you think, sweet-
heart?" Elli turned her conversation to the baby.

"What do you think is wrong?" Wyatt asked, putting the
coffee pot back on the burner.

A strange look passed over Elli's face, one that looked
like guilt and panic. But it was gone quickly. "I couldn't
say," she replied.

"But you were so good with her this afternoon." Wyatt
put his hands on his hips.

"Lucky, that's all. I just…remembered a few things."
The same strange look flitted over her features once more.

Wyatt took the coffee to the table. "You fooled me. You
looked like you knew exactly what you were doing." So
much so that Wyatt had felt completely inept. A feeling he
despised. He was used to being the one in control.

Elli and Darcy walked the length of the kitchen and
back. After a few moments, she admitted, "I haven't really
cared for a baby before. The things I thought of were simply
things I'd heard about. Not from experience, Mr. Black."

Her chin jutted up, closing the subject but making him

want to ask the questions now pulsing through his mind. But then he remembered the old saying—*Don't look a gift horse in the mouth*. He'd benefit from whatever insight she had and be glad of it.

"I don't really know what babies need," he said. "I fed her, patted her back like you did, walked her to sleep, but every time I put her down…"

Wyatt almost groaned. Of course. He'd forgotten one important thing. He'd been so focused on getting the formula the right temperature that he'd forgotten to check her diaper. Not that he had any clue what to do there either.

Pulling calves and shoveling out stalls was far less intimidating than one tiny newborn.

"She's probably due for a diaper change, isn't she." He tried to sound nonchalant. This was a perfect opportunity. Elli must know how to change a diaper. He could simply watch her so he'd know better for the next time.

Instead, Elli came around the corner of the counter and placed Darcy back in his arms. "Here you go, Uncle Wyatt," she said lightly. "You get diaper duty. I'll fix the coffee. Cream and sugar?"

Oh boy, Wyatt thought, looking down into Darcy's pursed face, his smug plan blown to smithereens. He was in for it now.

Will sparks fly between Elli and Wyatt?

Find out in
PROUD RANCHER, PRECIOUS BUNDLE

Available February 2011 from Harlequin Romance

Try these Healthy and Delicious Spring Rolls!

INGREDIENTS

2 packages rice-paper spring roll wrappers (20 wrappers)

1 cup grated carrot

¼ cup bean sprouts

1 cucumber, julienned

1 red bell pepper, without stem and seeds, julienned

4 green onions finely chopped— use only the green part

DIRECTIONS

1. Soak one rice-paper wrapper in a large bowl of hot water until softened.

2. Place a pinch each of carrots, sprouts, cucumber, bell pepper and green onion on the wrapper toward the bottom third of the rice paper.

3. Fold ends in and roll tightly to enclose filling.

4. Repeat with remaining wrappers. Chill before serving.

Find this and many more delectable recipes including the perfect dipping sauce in

YOUR BEST BODY NOW

by

TOSCA RENO

WITH STACY BAKER

Bestselling Author of **THE EAT-CLEAN DIET®**

Available wherever books are sold!

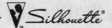

SPECIAL EDITION

FROM *USA TODAY* BESTSELLING AUTHOR

CHRISTINE RIMMER

COMES AN ALL-NEW BRAVO FAMILY TIES STORY.

Donovan McRae has experienced
the greatest loss a man can face, and
while he can't forgive himself, life—
and Abilene Bravo's love—are still
waiting for him. Can he find it in himself
to reach out and claim them?

Look for

DONOVAN'S CHILD

available February 2011

ROMANTIC
SUSPENSE

Sparked by Danger, Fueled by Passion.

NEW YORK TIMES BESTSELLING AUTHOR

RACHEL LEE

No Ordinary Hero

Strange noises...a woman's mysterious disappearance and a killer on the loose who's too close for comfort.

With no where else to turn, Delia Carmody looks to her aloof neighbour to help, only to discover that Mike Windwalker is no ordinary hero.

CONARD COUNTY *THE NEXT GENERATION*

Available in December.
Wherever books are sold.

USA TODAY bestselling author

Sharon Kendrick

introduces

HIS MAJESTY'S CHILD

The king's baby of shame!

King Casimiro harbors a secret—no one in the kingdom
of Zaffirinthos knows that a devastating accident has left
his memory clouded in darkness. And Casimiro himself
cannot answer why Melissa Maguire, an enigmatic English
rose, stirs such feelings in him…. Questioning his ability
to rule, Casimiro decides he will renounce the throne.
But Melissa has news she knows will rock the palace
to its core—*Casimiro has an heir!*

Law dictates Casimiro cannot abdicate, so he must find a
way to reacquaint himself with Melissa—his new queen!

Available from Harlequin Presents
February 2011

www.eHarlequin.com

HP12972